WITHDRAWN
FACTORY TOWN

Jon Bassoff

First Edition

Factory Town © 2014 by Jon Bassoff
All Rights Reserved.

A DarkFuse Release
www.darkfuse.com

Join the Newsletter:
http://eepurl.com/jOH5

Become a fan on Facebook:
www.facebook.com/darkfuse

Follow us on Twitter:
www.twitter.com/darkfuse

This book is a work of fiction. Names, characters, places and incidents are either a product of the author's imagination or are used fictitiously. Any resemblance to actual events, locales or persons, living or dead, is entirely coincidental.

For Tobey

Acknowledgements

First and foremost, I would like to thank Shane Staley, Greg Gifune, Dave Thomas, and the crew at DarkFuse for taking a chance in publishing a challenging novel like *Factory Town*. I would also like to thank the great Jack Reher, who is making a poor boy's dreams come true by adapting my novels for the big screen. And finally, I would like to thank my family for all the reasons that they know.

OTHER BOOKS BY AUTHOR

Corrosion (2013)

When we're asleep, nobody can tell
a sane man from an insane man.
— *Shock Corridor*

PROLOGUE

The house wasn't special, looked no different from every other house on the block, looked no different from every other house in the town. Two stories, beige paint, oversized garage, neatly trimmed lawn. A single light glowed dully in the upstairs bedroom; the rest of the house was dark. Across the street, a man sat inside a beat-up old Buick. His black hair was wild and disheveled, and his face was gaunt and pallid. He'd been sitting there for some time, gazing at the house through a rain-blurred windshield. Other than his tired car puffing exhaust, there were no other vehicles on the street, no signs of human life at all. A fellow could be excused for thinking that the Earth had died peacefully in its sleep...

Eventually, the man killed the engine, left the keys dangling. He pulled a flask from the glove compartment and took a long swallow, wiped his mouth

Factory Town

with the back of his hand. Then he reached into his jacket pocket, grabbed a cigarette and stuck it in his mouth. He pressed the cigarette to the car lighter and sucked deeply, the tobacco brightening all chimney-red. He smoked greedily, and within a few minutes the cigarette was down to the filter. He pushed open the door and threw the butt on the pavement. For a long time he sat there and watched the rain fall. And then, finally, he stepped outside and stood in the silent street with the silent houses.

He limped slowly across the yard and up the steps to the front porch, then stood there shivering, his eyes darting back and forth in their sockets. With trembling hands, he rang the doorbell, the sound echoing through the hallways. No movement inside, so he pounded on the door with the palm of his hand.

Lights began to turn on throughout the house. The sound of footsteps, and then the front door opened. An old woman stood behind the screen door, wearing a bathrobe, her gray hair matted from sleep. When she saw the stranger on the front porch, the color drained from her face. I...I thought you were my son, she said. Sometimes he comes when—

The man took a step forward, so that he was blocking the door. The woman stumbled backward, her bathrobe falling open, eyes petrified.

Where's the girl? he said.

What girl? I don't know. I—

The man pushed past the woman and entered the house. He stood there for a few moments, rocking back and forth, arms dangling at his side, and then he began pacing. Where's the girl? he said again. Where the fuck is she?

She shook her head. There's no girl here, she said. You must be confused. You must have the wrong address.

Shut up, he said. She's here somewhere. This is my house. This is where I live. Where have you hidden her?

For the next several minutes, the man searched the house, going into every room, pulling off covers and sheets, tearing apart desks and dressers and closets. And all the time he talked to himself, phrases inaudible, occasionally pausing to stomp his foot in frustration.

But the girl wasn't in the house. Nobody was, other than the old woman.

He returned to the living room and sat down on a chair. His lower lip was trembling, his left eye twitching. He rubbed his sickly face with his hands.

They're looking for me, he said, his voice barely louder than a whisper. Every damn one of them. And if they find me, I reckon they'll do some terrible things. They'll torture me. They'll bury me alive. They've done it to more than one man. But they ain't gonna find me. No, ma'am. I won't let 'em.

The man lifted his chin and stared at the woman who was now leaning against the wall, arms crossed, legs trembling badly.

I'd like a drink, he said. You got something?

Only...only wine.

Fine. Bring me the bottle.

She returned a moment later with a bottle of red wine, missing only a glass or two, and handed it to him. He yanked out the cork and placed the bottle to his mouth. He drank for a long time, until the bottle

Factory Town

was nearly empty. Then he stared straight ahead, his leathery face becoming more and more brooding. Outside the rain pounded on the asphalt and lightning flashed, no thunder.

I've done some terrible things, he said. Things that I ain't proud of, things that caused hurt.

The woman nodded her head then, in a small voice, said, It's okay. We've all done bad things.

The man gazed at the ground, clenched his fists. This house. I don't live here no more, do I? It was more of a statement than a question.

She shook her head. No, mister. I'm afraid not. I've lived here for six years now.

He nodded his head slowly, a sad smile appearing on his face. Six years, huh? Has it been that long?

Yes. My husband and I moved here from Pennsylvania. That was before he—

But the man wasn't listening, and suddenly he glanced around the room, eyes panicked. He got out of the chair and dropped to his knees, then to his stomach, ear pressed against the floor. He stayed like that for a long time, an expression of terror on his face. Can you hear 'em? he said. Well, can you? They're coming 'round the bend!

But there were no sounds other than a muted train horn somewhere in the distance. He jumped back to his feet and hurriedly strode to the window. He pulled the curtains back, gazed out the darkened glass. Turn out the lights, he said. Quick!

The woman did as she was told. They're coming, he said. And they've got torches and gunnysacks and rifles. What you learn is this: nobody really escapes in the end.

He glanced at the woman and then out the window. He closed the curtain and started pacing again, rubbing his hands together and muttering under his breath. Then, after some time, he stopped. Without warning, he reached beneath his shirt and pulled out a pistol. The woman gasped. He released the magazine, studied it for a long moment, and then jammed it back in place.

Let me ask you something, he said. You know who I am? You know what I done?

She shook her head. No. I—

You know what I done? And now he was shouting.

I don't...I don't know anything.

At this he nodded his head for a very long time. Then he placed the gun to his temple. This world and then the next, he said. He squeezed the trigger and there was a deafening explosion. He slumped to the floor, a hole in his temple, blood splattered across the carpet and the curtain and the wall.

Suddenly, everything was quiet. Everything but the sound of the clock. Hand still covering her mouth, the woman moved her head slowly and stared at the clock. She removed her hand from her mouth. It's 11:57, she whispered to nobody. Almost midnight. Then she turned back to the man, his face stilled in a grotesque expression. She stared at him for a long time. And then she saw him blink once and then once more...

CHAPTER 1

Darkness covered the city as I rested my head against a window, filthy rain trickling down my forehead. My reflection was that of a ghost, gaunt and pallid, my eyes the same as my father's. Speaking in a whisper: Oh Lord, forgive me. I have my share of regrets...

Factory Town. It was as if they had started demolishing the entire city, building by building, house by house, and then had decided it wasn't worth the effort, let it die on its own terms. There was crumbling concrete and collapsed fences, broken glass and discarded furniture. Brick buildings worn down from time and neglect, the windows boarded up and covered with graffiti. A bank clock, both hands missing. Dumpsters upturned. Fire escapes fallen to the ground. Rubble everywhere. A church, vandalized and rotted. And from somewhere, the strange echoes

Factory Town

of a laugh track. I had heard once that laugh tracks were mostly made forty, fifty years ago, so it was the laughter of the dead.

A loud crashing sound startled me. I looked up and saw a mess of a woman appear from the doorway of a building. She wore a torn men's dress shirt, a frayed jean skirt, and a pair of pink cowboy boots. Her bleached blonde hair was cut short and ragged, and a wounded cigarette dangled from her purple lips. She walked with a slight limp. She might have been twenty or fifty; her face and body had seen better days. When she saw me, she sneered, said, I know you. You're the fellow they been talking about.

I shook my head. You must be mistaken, I said. I just arrived in town.

No. I ain't mistaken. You're the one. You got a name?

Russell Carver. And you must have confused me with somebody else.

Well, shit. Maybe. It don't matter none. Besides, you're a cute one. You looking for a date?

I didn't know how to respond, so I didn't say a word. She grinned a mean grin, cleared her throat, and spat on the ground. Then she started walking. Lonely and disoriented, I followed.

Through the broken streets we walked. We came upon filthy blankets, an old shattered bathtub, and a rusty shovel. A single army boot and a string of Christmas lights. She leaned up against me, placing her head on my shoulder, her arm intertwined with mine. And a man leaning against a building, getting soaked in the rain, gray hair slicked into a sloppy pompadour, shouted out, Don't go with that woman, she'll steal your heart, yes she will! and the whore shook her head and said, Hush, and we kept walking, and the rain was falling, and the buildings were collapsing, and my brain was bleeding.

Soon we were inside a skeleton of a building, and I followed her through a series of strange corridors and into a darkened room, colder than outside. She pulled me tight and laughed, and it was a terrible laugh. She smelled of cheap perfume and cheaper booze. I felt disgusted and disdainful, anxious and apprehensive. The room itself was stark and filthy with a single light bulb dangling from the ceiling, the mattress stained with blood and bourbon, the wall stuffed with asbestos. And on the nightstand, a clock badly decayed, the numbers peeling, the hands forever stuck three minutes before twelve...

Glancing out the window, I saw several strange-looking men in bulging parkas skulking around the perimeter, constantly, methodically. I pulled the curtain shut and leaned against the wall. My temple was pounding.

Meanwhile, the whore didn't waste any time. She pulled off her shirt, revealing large, disfigured breasts, and then she rubbed them, but there was nothing sensual about it. She asked me what I wanted, went through a list of carnal acts with alarming indifference, but I remained clothed, told her that I'd pay her fairly, that I only wanted someone to talk to, perhaps someone to hold, so that I could get some sleep. At that she smirked, but she consented, money is money after all, and while she smoked cigarettes down to the filter and slugged peppermint schnapps from a green army thermos, I got to the business at

Factory Town

hand, told her about Alana, about the mysterious circumstances of her disappearance, long and detailed as they were — six years searching through cities and deserts and mountains. I didn't leave out a single detail, but the whore had vacant eyes, both bloodshot, and it was obvious that she was bored by my story, slumping down against the wall, her head lolling back and forth, not showing any real comprehension, as if I were talking in a foreign language, when in reality I spoke in measured tones, despite my insomnia, a month or more without sleep...

So to try to interest her, I pulled out a photograph and showed it to her, a computer-generated image showing the way Alana might look today: a young girl with a mess of dirty blonde hair, a pink mouth, and blue eyes deadly serious. At this, the whore's head finally stopped lolling, and her eyes connected with mine, those bloodshot eyes, ravaged by drink and whoredom, and she mockingly asked if I was a detective or something, and I said no, that I was just an ordinary fellow who looked out for the most vulnerable among us, and certainly this girl Alana was vulnerable.

I have sources, I said, reliable sources, and they tell me that she's here in Factory Town, but she's in great danger, doesn't have long to live. The whore studied the photograph for some time and then shook her head. Nope. Never seen her before. Never seen her in my whole life. But I noticed that her mouth twitched, a liar's tic.

She crushed out another cigarette and stared into my eyes, unblinking. She was lowdown and spiteful, that much was clear, and she knew more than she was letting on to...

In the room next to ours, a couple was shouting in Chinese or Japanese, violence ready to ensue. Suddenly I felt tired, so goddamned tired. This investigation, this insomnia, was getting to be too much...

So how long you been here then? she said. In Factory Town, I mean.

It's hard to say. Not long. A day maybe. A week perhaps.

She laughed harshly. I figured so much. Otherwise you woulda known.

Would have known what?

Woulda known that you ain't different from the rest of us. Woulda known that you ain't gonna find nothing here. Woulda known you ain't gonna find that girl.

I gritted my teeth, clenched my fists. How do you know that? Have you seen her? What do you know?

What I know don't matter. It don't matter at all.

What the hell do you mean by that?

She grinned, baring a set of rotten brown teeth. What I mean is that I heard your story a million times before. It's always the same. Always the same goddamn thing.

And now I could feel that old familiar rage, but I kept it together. She's here, I said. In this town. My sources—

Fuck your sources!

The shouting in the next room was getting louder and louder, and bottles were shattering, one after another.

Goddamn, little boy, she said, booze and saliva spraying from her filthy mouth. Don't you know

Factory Town

where you are? Don't you know what'll become of you? This here is a town of sin, a town of sadness, a town of hatred. Every damn person guilty of something. Every damn person afraid to talk. Do you hear me, Mr. Carver? A million goddamn secrets buried beneath the dirt and rubble. You gonna go digging? Well then. You gonna find some beating hearts in those corpses...

Outside the rain pounded on the asphalt, and lightning flashed, no thunder. And now I'd heard just about enough. I rose to my feet, ready to storm out, but suddenly the room was spinning like crazy, and the single light bulb shattered to the floor. Panicked, I grabbed on to the metal chair, holding on for dear life. The whore stood in front of me, laughing. With great purpose, she yanked off her skirt, swayed her hips, then began sticking her fingers inside her cunt, one at a time, slowly and systematically. I felt repulsed, but I watched as her entire hand was swallowed up, and then she began with the other hand...

She puckered her diseased lips, said, Watcha gonna do, Mr. Carver? Who you gonna love?

The spinning room finally coming to a stop, I pushed my way past the whore and shouldered open the door. The photograph was still in my hand, now badly crumpled. As I staggered down the hallway, I could hear the whore's laughter echoing across the linoleum...

* * *

The hallway was dark and terrible, what with all the dead birds on the ground, dozens of them, and worse still, a few of them alive, but barely, wings flapping almost imperceptibly, willing themselves to fly, without any success. Graffiti covered the walls, a series of violent messages. And on the ceiling, an elaborate mural of a young woman, expression serious, bits and pieces of her face peeling and falling like confetti to the floor.

    I walked with my head down, mumbling to myself, trying to put the pieces together, so many pieces, all jagged, and the hallway stretched forever, a long corridor, winding in a mazelike fashion. I wandered along for what seemed like days, becoming increasingly disoriented, hateful images crashing around my skull like blind birds in a cage. I could hear the muted sounds of conversation but didn't see any people. At times the conversation would fade away completely, but then it would return, get louder and louder, and I could pick out fragments, but none of it had any meaning for me, none of it made any sense: *hide the rest in those mason jars...all those corpses in the cavern...do you think he'll find out?... what about him?... do you think he'll find out?*

    And then the conversation faded away for good, and I continued walking, and I came across a group of old men, huddled around a trashcan filled with fire, rubbing their hands together, shadows flickering across the cement wall. My footsteps echoed loudly, but the men didn't look up, so focused on their own hushed conversation. I tried asking for help, for directions out of the building, but there was no response, mutes to my voice. And then, from the corner of my eye, I saw what appeared to be a small caped figure dart across the corridor, just a momentary flash, and

Factory Town

melt into the concrete wall.

For several moments, I doubted my own senses, doubted that I had indeed seen anything. After all, I hadn't slept in so many days and my own perceptions tended to be faulty, fading in and out and in again like a radio signal on a county line road.

Slowly, I edged across the corridor, past the old men huddled around the trashcan, past a young woman with a tattoo sleeve and dreadlocked hair, past a mangy calico cat, and I came to the wall and saw that there was a metallic door, and on the door a makeshift sign in the jagged scrawl: the Annihilator Waits Here.

CHAPTER 2

Nobody seemed to notice I was there, nobody said a word, so I pulled open the door and started down the long staircase. All was darkness, and I walked deeper and deeper underground, the stairs winding back and forth and back again, the shrieks of rats and the sound of my own shoes echoing against the concrete. I shone a cheap Bic lighter, but there was an icy draft and it kept flickering out. Cautiously, I maneuvered down the crumbling stairs, gripping onto the metal handrail for support, but after a while the handrail twisted into nothingness, and I lost my grip on the lighter; I was a blind man, waiting to step off a concrete cliff.

With great trepidation, I put one foot in front of the other, one foot in front of the other, and I went farther and farther into the pit, feeling like hours were passing, but not knowing for sure, and finally,

Factory Town

when I was filled with fear and despair, I saw the distant glow of a light down just a ways.

I quickened my pace, and soon the staircase ended and I came upon a rotted wooden door hanging on by its hinges. I kicked it open with my foot, the door splintering apart. It led into a corridor, the walls covered with more violent graffiti, the floors with sawdust, broken glass, dead rodents, and bullet casings. It was difficult to breathe, the air contaminated.

And then down a ways, the hallway opened into an expansive room, lit only by a series of flashlights shining from various positions on the floor. The walls were covered with plaster, much of it peeling away revealing the original brick. In the middle of the room were 25-30 rows of splintered wooden seats, separated by red-carpeted aisles. The ceiling was dome-shaped, decorated with elaborate mosaics, worn but still visible. And in the back of the room a balcony, nearly collapsed, held up by five metal poles jutting from the floor. At some point it must have been some type of a theatre, but now there was no stage, no movie screen, just dirt and rubble everywhere.

I stood there for a long time, confused and disoriented. I took a few steps forward. Once I got over the shock, there was a kind of beauty in this decay. I breathed slowly, deeply, body relaxing.

I walked farther into the room and stood in front of the theatre seats. Then I sat down. I stared straight ahead, ghosts of days past drifting in front of my face, smiling, not sad. I closed my eyes. Soon I was drifting off to sleep...

I didn't dream. Maybe I didn't sleep after all. I felt somebody tapping me on my shoulder. Then I heard a voice, strangely familiar. What are you doing here, mister? How'd you find out about all of this?

I turned around and saw a boy, no more than eight or nine years old. He was dressed as a superhero, black tights, red shirt, yellow cape. The cape had an oversized A made out of duct tape, colored red and beginning to peel off. On his face he wore a black mask, one of those cheap plastic ones, held onto his head with a rubber band.

I...I saw you in the hallway. I was curious. I followed you.

You shouldn't have done that. I could've killed you. Why'd you do that?

Because...I wanted to talk to you.

So you don't work for the Cowboy, then?

The Cowboy? Who's the Cowboy?

You can't tell anybody about this hideaway, he said. Or else everything would be ruined. All our plans.

No. Of course not.

Showing no fear, the boy sat down next to me on one of the theatre seats. He had pitch-black hair and a sad mouth. One of his eyes twitched from time to time.

So you must be the Annihilator, I said.

No answer for a while, then: Yes.

A lot of bad guys in this town?

He only nodded his head.

And there must be some good guys, too. Guys you're protecting.

He thought for a moment. A few, he said. Not many though. More bad guys than good guys.

Yes, I said. That seems to be the way of the world.

Factory Town

We sat there for a long time, and it was awfully strange being in an old abandoned movie theatre in an old abandoned apartment building talking to the Annihilator, the first superhero I'd ever met.

What about weapons? I said. Do you have any? To fight the bad guys, I mean.

He nodded. Oh, yes. I've got weapons. I've got lots of weapons.

And at that, he walked a few rows back and reached under the seat and pulled out a cardboard box decorated with his signature A. Inside there were shields and swords and guns and daggers, all plastic, and I nodded my head and said, You're well prepared. I can see why you're the protector.

These weapons are fine, he said, but I'd like me a real gun and a real sword. Then I'd feel safer.

What about your parents? Where are they? Do they know you're down here? This doesn't seem like the kind of place where children should be playing, you know? Just look all around you. Broken glass. Dead animals. Bullet casings.

The boy shook his head. This is where we hide. There is more than just me here. There are a hundred at least. We've got our own little world down here. It's great. We play games. Marbles. Cops and robbers. Cowboys and Indians. And no grown-up can ever tell us what to do. It's our own little world, you see.

A hundred kids you say? Well, where are they? I don't see anybody besides you.

He smiled and shook his head. Oh, there are lots of places to hide.

Yeah? Why are they hiding?

Jon Bassoff

He paused for a long time. Because they're scared of you.

Scared of me? That doesn't make any sense. I just arrived here. I'm a stranger. They don't know me.

Oh, they're scared of you. Why wouldn't they be scared of you? Why wouldn't they? You do terrible things. You're just like my father. You even look like him. You have the same eyes. My father is a terrible person. Everybody says so. Do you know what my father did?

I'm a stranger, I said. You don't know me. Those kids don't know me.

He chained me to a radiator. Because I was bothering him. Just because I was bothering him. Left me with a bowl of water, like a dog. All the kids say that was a terrible thing. And what he did to my mom was even worse. But at least he gave me these marbles. That was good of him. Some fathers wouldn't even do that.

At that moment, he noticed the photograph crumpled in my hand. Watcha got there, mister? Who's that a photograph of?

I released my grip and handed it to the boy. He looked at the picture intently.

Her name is Alana, I said. She went missing years ago. This is how she might look today. There haven't been many leads. The police sort of gave up. It's a shame. There's so much crime nowadays. It's my job to find her. I've been looking for more than six years. My sources tell me that she's here, in Factory Town.

She looks familiar, the boy said. I think I've played with her before.

I squatted down until I was face to face with the

Factory Town

boy. Tell me more. You say you've played with her?

Yes. That is, I can't be sure, but I think...

Where? When? This is very important, you see. Any information would be helpful. Any information at all. I've had some leads, but this...

It was cops and robbers. That's right. She was the new girl. But she wanted to be a princess. The game wouldn't have worked. The new kids always have to be the robbers. Those are the rules. We kept telling her. She should have listened to us. We've been here forever. We've paid our dues.

I pressed him further, but he couldn't/wouldn't give me any more information.

Just do me a favor, I said. If you see her again, let her know I'm looking for her. My name is Russell Carver. She'll know me by name.

He nodded his head, but now his eyes were blank, his jaw slack.

Well, I guess I'll be going now. I've got a few leads that I need to follow up on...

But the kid was in his own world now, staring straight ahead. Slowly, he rose from his seat and walked toward the back of the theatre, gripping a sword in one hand and a shield in the other. He took a few more steps forward then started swinging his sword back and forth, apparently engaged in an imaginary battle with one of the bad guys he'd referenced...

And this bad guy's name was Dr. Devil, and he was a member of the Red Alliance's inner circle. He was a brutal hulk of a man with thick tattooed arms, leathery skin, a badly scarred face, and red horns protruding from his skull. He was a killer through and through (who could forget the brutal assassination of Leopard Man, or the way he'd ripped the beating heart from the ribcage of The Blue Bullet), and he wanted nothing more than to add the Annihilator to his list of victims.

He went after our hero with unbridled passion and hatred, throwing spears and daggers and fireballs. But the Annihilator was too quick, dodging the projectiles with great precision, doing flips and cartwheels to stay out of harm's way. In the background, full orchestration music. And then, with the strength and power of a million men, the Annihilator charged toward Dr. Devil and slammed into his chin with his fist, sending him hurtling to the cement floor. Without hesitation, the Annihilator, the protector of Factory Town, drew his sword (a gift from Sir Lancelot himself), placed the tip of his blade to his opponent's throat and said, barely louder than a whisper: Time to die, Devil Boy!

But Dr. Devil only laughed. Die? he said. You don't have the guts! Hell, you couldn't even protect your mother, your own mother! Yes, yes, I was in your house with you as she was punched and kicked, tortured and maimed, a bloody miscarriage. And you just stood by and watched, piss rolling down your leg! And I was in your house with you when she stopped eating, starved herself, ended up nothing more than a skeleton. You're a goddamn coward, you hear me? You didn't have the guts to take on your father, and you don't have the guts to take on Dr. Devil!

Dr. Devil was wrong.

With a sudden brutality, the Annihilator jammed

Factory Town

the sword into the monster's throat, left it there for a long moment, and then yanked it out. He watched dispassionately as life came leaking out. Dr. Devil, still flesh and blood, tried grasping a hold of his throat, tried closing the wound, but it was no use. Time passed, and he twitched violently, his bloody tongue bloated in his mouth, and then finally he was still, his soul sucked violently into the fiery furnaces.

The Annihilator raised his scarlet sword and stuck it back into the holster. He wiped his brow and looked up to the heavens. Lord, he had it coming, he whispered.

Shocked by the spectacle, I walked quietly past the boy toward the staircase. He never saw me leave, or if he did, he never said a word.

CHAPTER 3

I ascended the stairs quickly, breathing heavily from the exertion. Strange sounds echoed in the stairway: a woman singing opera, the laugh track of a sitcom, the clacking of a typewriter. Finally, I came to a door and pushed it open, but as I walked through the corridor, it soon became obvious that I was on the wrong floor. Feeling that familiar sense of dread, I wandered aimlessly through the darkened corridor, searching for an exit out of the building, becoming increasingly frustrated by the numerous dead ends and mock doors. On more than one occasion I did find a door that actually opened, but each time it turned out to be a supplies closet or a furnace room.

And so time passed that way, until eventually, to my great relief, I saw the unmistakable glimmer of light, the dust rising like some spectral vision. I pushed open the heavy steel door and stepped outside.

Factory Town

I breathed deeply. Looking around, it was clear that I was back in the town's center, but now everything looked different somehow, and I felt, once again, like a stranger.

The exterior of the building that I exited from now resembled a derelict hospital. Three-stories, gray brick, with chimneystacks rising from each corner of the gable roof. Wings jutted from the main block and were covered with dying ivy. Many of the windows were broken, and all were barred. And beyond the building, rising like a beacon, the factory, all twisted metal and catwalks and winding cylinders and smokestacks.

I stood there for a long time, just staring at the factory, mesmerized. By all appearances it was deserted, abandoned, but as I stood there, the sickle of a moon and a few dead stars my only light, I could see the faint tendrils of smoke rising from the stacks. I felt a coldness rise up inside of me, a coldness that I knew would never leave me, and I stared at the factory, and I knew something was happening in there, something terrible, and I knew that every secret in the world was hidden in the factory's walls, and I had to find out, had to find out...

It was late at night or early in the morning, and I was hungry and tired. I wandered down the splintered streets and sidewalks, all covered with shattered bottles and foreign newspapers and dead birds and worn-out shoes. My eyes stayed focused on the factory, but no matter how long I walked it remained out of reach, off in the distance.

My thoughts turned inward and I thought about my task, finding the girl, and I worried that they had thrown her into the industrial lake or, worse yet, buried her in the cement. And so I wandered through the town, lost in my own anxieties, going round and round in circles, and when I looked up I realized that I'd lost sight of the factory, lost sight of the town's center completely. Trying to regain my bearings, I saw that I was now in an old and rundown residential neighborhood. A cold wind was blowing, and a few tired cottonwoods swayed lazily. There was a row of dark one-story brick ranches, the lawns nothing but dirt and weeds. Somewhere some cats were fighting to the death. A tin can clanked down the pavement, paused at my feet, and then continued on its way.

I was lost. I thought about walking toward one of the houses and knocking on the door, but I feared that whoever opened the door would be armed with a rifle or a handgun, and me with nothing.

And then I heard the faint sounds of music. At first I thought it was just my imagination, but as I moved forward, the music became louder, more distinct. It sounded like '50s do-wop, and I could also hear the echoes of laughter.

I quickened my pace. Following the music, I walked across a lawn littered with beer cans and machinery. Out of the darkness, a pit-bull barked and growled, made like he was going to chomp through my leg, but he was chained to a post and didn't do anything but choke himself as he lunged forward. I leaped over the fence and continued through a frozen dirt field and along a little gully until up ahead I saw a big farmhouse, its windows all lit up, the music filling the night sky.

Wide-eyed and slack-jawed, I took another step

Factory Town

forward, but I tripped, nearly falling face first into the frozen field. I pushed myself up to my knees and turned around. I saw that I had tripped over the legs of a man. He was propped up against a tree, his head slumped forward. I was sure he was dead.

He wore overalls and no jacket despite the frigid weather, 20 degrees at most. His face was pallid and waxy looking. I kneeled next to him, said, You all right, mister? No response. I moved closer still and tapped his knee. Mister? Still nothing. I studied his chest, his shoulders, his mouth for any signs of breath, but saw none.

I sat on my haunches, took a few deep breaths, thought things over. Everything about this town was strange; nothing made any sense. What would happen if I approached the house and told them that there was a dead man in the field? Would they peg me as the killer? These types of towns don't like outsiders, that much is sure. Would they call the cops, an ambulance? Did they even have a police force in this town?

I rose to my feet, unsteadily. And that's when the dead man's head jerked upward, his eyelids fluttered open, and his lips curled into a grin.

Christ, Russell, he said. You look as if you've seen a ghost.

I was rattled badly, and I scurried backwards. Long moments passed and the man just kept on grinning. And then, finally, recognition. It was Charlie Gardner, a childhood friend who I hadn't seen in years. I breathed deeply, relieved.

Charlie? I said. What are you doing here?

He grinned again, and then shook his head. Ah, I

was just goofing with you, buddy. I came out here for a breath of fresh air and saw you wandering along, and I figured I'd give you a scare. Got you good, huh?

Well, sure. But I mean, what are you doing here in Factory Town?

Charlie narrowed his eyes and shook his head. What are you talking about, Russell? I never left Factory Town. Well, except for a couple years in the army. That was a hell of a thing, buddy, a hell of a thing. I killed a man. Can you believe it? Shot him right in the chest. Never thought I'd kill anyone…

I gestured toward the lit-up house, the music and laughter louder than ever. What's going on in there? I asked. Some sort of a party?

Party? No, not exactly. Cards night. We play every Tuesday. Half the town shows up. Even the Vultures.

The Vultures?

It's low stakes, Russell. Twenty bucks and you're in. Say, why don't you join us? It's a good time, real good time. We don't have many good times in this town. I can introduce you to some important people.

I don't know, I said. I should probably get back to town, find a place to lay my head. I haven't slept in a long time. I need to get some rest so I can continue my investigation.

Charlie pulled back his greasy blonde hair with his hand, thought things over for a few minutes. Need a place to crash, huh? Well, hell, Russell, I got plenty of space at my place. And I live right here in the neighborhood. You remember my house, don't you?

I didn't know what he was talking about, but I didn't want to let on. Sure, I said. I remember it well.

Factory Town

Well, it's settled then. We'll play a few hands of cards, drink some Tennessee white whiskey, and then crash at my place. Now that I think of it, you can share a room with my mother. You remember my mother, don't you, pal?

Well, sure.

She's changed a lot. She's not the woman you remember. She's sick, very sick.

I'm sorry to hear that.

It's a mental disease. Nothing anybody can do. You feel so helpless. They can fix a broken leg, but when a person's mind is broken...

We walked slowly toward the house, Charlie pausing every few minutes to take a nibble from a metal flask. I watched as the moon vanished into the fog and mist. The gravel crunched beneath our shoes. When Charlie spoke again, his voice was hushed and conspiratorial. So tell me, Russell. You ever settle down? Ever find a girl?

Yes, Charlie. I got married for a spell.

But?

The marriage didn't last. What does?

Only damnation, Russell.

We arrived at the house. A nearly collapsed picket fence surrounded the property, the white paint peeling, the wraparound porch rotting and sagging. The old farmhouse had been left to fend for itself and had long since given up. But tonight the house was alive, what with the light and music and laughter.

I walked a step behind as Charlie made his way across the lawn and toward the front porch where five men and a single woman—her teeth missing, hair thinning—were drinking whiskey and talking about cars. When they saw me, conversation ceased and they eyed me suspiciously, always the outsider.

Charlie said: Folks, this is Russell Carver, an old buddy of mine. We had us some good times, yes sir, we did. He's visiting Factory Town for a spell and it would be awfully kind of you if you made him feel at home. Like I said, he's an old buddy of mine.

Pleasure, I said, and they all nodded their heads in unison. For a while we stood there awkwardly, nobody saying a thing, then one of the men, a skinny fellow with one eye, one leg, but thank goodness two arms, said, Watcha doing here in Factory Town, mister?

I'm investigating a disappearance, I said. A girl named Alana. She's been missing for some time. I have reliable sources that say she's here, in Factory Town. So far I haven't had any success in locating her.

You a detective then?

No, not exactly. I—

I ain't never heard of no gal named Alana, said another man, corncob pipe in his mouth, skin as white as a ghost. And I woulda 'membered that name, sure as shit.

I've got a photograph, I said. Computer generated. The way she might look today. Mind taking a look?

I pulled out the tattered photograph and handed it to the skinny man, who proceeded to pass it around the group. Each person held the photograph, but not one person looked at it.

Nope, said the ghost man. None of us ever seen her, and that's a fact. Best you go looking somewhere

Factory Town

else. Like I said, I woulda remembered her had I seen her. But I ain't never. None of us have.

You didn't even glance at the photo, I said. Not one of you.

Now that ain't fair, said the skinny one. We all looked at it, of course we did!

She's in danger, I said, grave danger, and I'm not going to be able to save her if you're all hiding something or if you're all protecting somebody.

There were a few long moments of silence before the woman spoke: Mr. Carver, we're not hiding a thing. There's nothing to hide. It's you that's doing the concealing. Don't think you're so clever. We can see right through you. Anybody with an ounce of sense could.

I snatched the photograph out of the woman's hand and stuck it back in my jacket pocket. I was angry, but I kept it together.

I said: We've all got secrets, I guess, and that seemed to placate the bastards. Charlie grabbed my shoulder and we walked across the porch, the screen door hanging off its hinges, banging open and shut, and pushed our way inside.

The house was filled with people milling around, drinking beer and whiskey, slapping each other on the back, dancing haphazardly. The music that I'd assumed was coming from the radio was actually coming from a makeshift stage where four blacks in matching purple zoot suits played a cappella.

Looking around, I saw that there was no furniture, no carpet, no photographs. Several of the windows were busted out. In the kitchen, the refrigerator and oven were both beyond repair, doors missing, wires splayed every which way.

Charlie walked me around, introducing me to people whose names I forgot the moment he said them. He grabbed me a Coca-Cola from a cabinet and then disappeared into the crowd, while I stood around, not sure of what to do with myself.

Eventually, I sat down in the corner, exhausted again, listened to the music and drank my soda. People walked past me, stepped over me. I pulled out the photograph and stared at the image once again. And now I noticed that the photograph had changed. Alana's face, which for such a long time had possessed an expression of innocent joy, had now transformed into that of terror, eyes open wide, mouth shaped in a silent scream. And, if you looked very carefully, stared at the photograph for a long enough time, you could see, standing directly behind the girl, the vague silhouette of a man.

CHAPTER 4

Hope faded fast, so I changed from soda to whiskey, while the black men picked up instruments and the music changed from do-wop to swamp blues. The sound was scary, like skeletons clattering on a ship deck, and the dancing intensified, bodies convulsing wildly. Men pounded the floor hard with their feet, fired Mexican *pistolas* into the air. Women unbuttoned the tops of their dresses, revealing cleavage wet with perspiration. Eight or more people were passed out on the floor, and I had to step over them to move across the room. A blond man wearing an Indian headdress grabbed and hugged me; a gypsy woman wearing a live cobra stuck her tongue down my throat. My head was spinning out of control.

I saw strange things. I saw beautiful young women smoking kinnikinnick from a Sun Drop soda can. I saw a pair of old men, arms tied tightly with belts, shooting up scopolamine. I saw a transvestite sucking off a midget, a religious fanatic chewing on broken glass, a sword swallower bleeding from the mouth. I saw books burning orange in a makeshift bonfire, scandalous paintings being slashed with a rusty nail, violins being shattered with a nightstick. I saw mania filling the eyes of each and every person: the man with a hundred piercings, the woman with the skeletal face, the girl with the haunted smile, etc. etc. I saw recklessness, hunger, and desperation. I saw the decline of humanity.

I was lost, lost, lost, as always, lost.

Charlie Gardner appeared from behind a curtain, as if he'd been standing there his whole life. There are some people you should meet, he said. They're expecting you.

Expecting me? It made no sense. Nobody knew me here. I was a stranger.

I followed Charlie up a winding staircase crowded with carousers and degenerates. Some of them pointed at me and laughed. Others just sighed and shook their heads. There was barely any room to ascend the stairs, and I found myself stepping on feet and knees, and knocking over drinks.

We finally made it upstairs, and Charlie closed the door behind me. Everything was suddenly quiet, the shouts and laughter and music muted. We walked down the long hallway. Water dripped from the ceiling. One of the doors slammed open and a woman staggered out of the room, her black hair short and unkempt, her face wind-chapped and spiteful. She wore a short flower dress, all tattered and torn, and one of her high-heel shoes was missing. Walking next

Factory Town

to her was a young man who looked even more disheveled than she. He wore no shoes, no shirt, and his face was hidden by long, filthy hair. He was puffing on a thin cigar. I couldn't take my eyes off of him.

What you looking at, nigga? he said.

Nothing, I said. I'm looking at nothing.

He and the girl kept walking, but he stopped every three or four steps to turn around and glare at me. He mouthed something: I know you.

Charlie opened a door and we entered a room filled with smoke. The floor was black parquet. The walls were red brick. In the middle of the room was a long sheet of corrugated metal held up by stacks of whiskey crates. Three men sat around the makeshift table in plastic lawn chairs, playing cards. They didn't look up when we entered, didn't look up when Charlie introduced me.

One of the men was tall and flag pole skinny with damp black hair falling below his eyebrows. His face was pale and sickly-looking, beads of sweat forming at his temples. Another one of the men looked much more vigorous with a barrel chest and square jaw, a Fu-Manchu mustache visible above a week of growth on his face. He wore a Stetson hat, tilted upward on the back of his head. The other man was small and old with thinning white hair and a pair of spectacles resting on the tip of his rosacea nose.

The doctor, the sheriff, and the pastor, Charlie whispered to me. It's like the start of a fucking joke, you know?

They played cards and nobody talked. I couldn't figure out the game. Each of them stared at their cards for a long time and then somebody would pick a card from the deck, throw down one from their hand. It wasn't poker. It wasn't blackjack. It wasn't any card game I'd ever played.

From the back of the room, a phone started ringing. There was no reaction. The phone rang and rang, fifteen times at least. Nobody moved.

The fellow with the Stetson hat (the sheriff?) spoke: So this is the new fellow, huh? He didn't look up, remained focused on his hand—an ace of diamonds, three of hearts, eight of clubs, ten of hearts, and a jack of spades.

His name is Russell Carver, Charlie said. We go way back; ain't that right, Russell?

I nodded my head yes.

Now the old man spoke. Have a seat, Russell. Take a load off. I glanced at his gnarled hands. Tattoo letters across each finger: Jesus Lives. This was the man of religion.

There was an empty chair, so I sat down. Charlie remained standing. The phone rang again, this time only two rings before ceasing. The sickly doctor dealt me a hand of cards. Was there a game, or were they just flipping cards to pass the time? Three kings and a pair of queens. The men stared at me. I dropped one of the kings on the jagged metal table, drew a four of diamonds.

This is the way it went for some time. We played cards and nobody talked. The game kept going. There would be no winner. The game kept going. And the phone rang again.

Finally, conversation. This time, the doctor spoke. His voice was high and reedy. He was sweating profusely. His left eye was amblyopic. This town, he

Factory Town

said, isn't for everybody. There's a lot of...misery.

I stayed focused on my cards, didn't say a word.

Indeed, said the pastor. Sometimes I wonder if Factory Town isn't some sort of a purgatory. Sometimes I wonder if it isn't Hell. Then he smiled. But no, that can't be. After all, we're all alive, aren't we? Flesh and blood. Even the Vultures are alive. Isn't that so, Estaban?

I looked up and saw the man whom he was referring to huddled in the corner of the room. I hadn't noticed him before. He was dressed in the rags of a beggar. He had a long black beard and long greasy hair. His skin was covered with lesions, and his eyes bulged wildly. He was tall but he couldn't have weighed more than 100 pounds. He was gnawing greedily on a piece of meat, shielding his precious food with his arms. When the pastor spoke to him, he only grunted a response.

The gentlemen playing cards all looked at each other knowingly. Then the sheriff tipped his hat and said, You ever met, Estaban, Mr. Carver? One of Factory Town's finest.

No sir, I said.

Come here, Estaban, the sheriff said. I want you to meet Russell Carver.

Estaban, the beggar, didn't respond, just continued attacking the meat. The sheriff tipped his Stetson hat, then pulled out his Smith and Wesson. He cocked the pistol and pointed it directly at Estaban. Come here, old man, he said, before I blow your goddamn brains across them there red bricks.

The ragged old man thought things over for a few moments and then pushed himself to his feet. He

Jon Bassoff

kept the piece of meat cradled in his arms and, struggling to maintain his balance, walked slowly toward the table. The sheriff pulled up a chair and Estaban the Beggar sat down.

Estaban rocked back and forth and mumbled some nonsense. The doctor patted his hand, looked up at me. Such a tragedy, the doctor said. A goddamn leper in this day and age. We've treated him with mercury and viper's flesh, but no success.

Is he contagious? I asked.

We're all contagious, the doctor said.

The sheriff tossed his cards on the table, nodded at the leper. Look at this piece of shit, he said, munching away happily, ignoring our guest completely. You hungry, Mr. Carver?

Yes, I said. I haven't had a thing to eat since I arrived here.

Food is hard to come by, the pastor said. No farming. No livestock. Here in Factory Town a can of beans is worth more than gold.

Hear that? the sheriff said, grabbing the leper's shoulder and digging in with his fingers until he cried out in pain. Our guest is hungry. How about sharing some of that meat with him?

Estaban squirmed away from the lawman's grip. My food, he said. Always my food.

He's hungry, the sheriff said. He ain't gonna eat all your food, so just relax. Just a few bites, understand.

I stared at the bloody piece of flesh and shook my head. I'll wait, I said. No need for me to take somebody else's food.

But the sheriff only glared at me and snarled.

Factory Town

You'll eat, he said. Goddamn it, you'll eat.

And then, just like that, a metal plate with a piece of bloody flesh, and he'd said there was no livestock in this town.

You'll eat, the sheriff said again. By fuck, you'll eat every piece of this here delicacy.

Things got out of control quickly. Before I could react, the pastor and the doctor grabbed a hold of me and pulled back my arms, and the sheriff picked up a chunk of the bloody flesh and attempted to shove it into my mouth. Like an uncooperative toddler, I clenched my mouth shut and started kicking wildly. Despite the two of them restraining me, I was strong enough to pull free, and I tried getting out of my seat, but then my old friend Charlie was there again, and he was helping the doctor and the pastor, and they pinned me on the ground. The sheriff stood over me, cocked his pistol, and pointed it at my forehead. I stopped fighting then.

Meanwhile, Estaban the Beggar was good and angry about his food being stolen, and he was rocking back and forth, raising his diseased arms to the heavens and moaning and crying.

The sheriff, that mean son-of-a-bitch, got down on his haunches and told me to open up. I glared at him for a moment, but that gun remained steady in his hand, so I opened my mouth and he pushed some of the bloody meat inside. Think of it as your initiation, he said.

I chewed slowly, disdainfully, while the men stood over me, grotesque grins spread across each of their faces. Estaban continued crying. The meat tasted awful—I think it was rotten—but I managed to swallow it down without gagging. When I was finished, Charlie helped me to my feet and each of the men patted me on the back and rubbed my shoulder, and they were laughing like it was all one big fucking joke.

Did you see the expression on his face? the doctor said. Priceless.

He took it better than most, the sheriff said. I'll give him that much.

I told you he was good folk, Charlie said. Salt of the Earth.

A good lad, the pastor agreed.

But my expression must have revealed my rage because Charlie looked at me and said, Ah, take it easy, Russell. It was just a little joke we like to play on outsiders. That meat ain't gonna hurt you, none. Ostrich meat, that's all it is. It ain't no big deal, so don't act like it is.

While Charlie was talking, I suddenly remembered Alana, and my throat tightened. Here I was playing cards and eating ostrich while that little girl's life was in danger (if she wasn't dead already). I could feel tears making their way to my eyes. Everything was wrong. I reached into my pocket for the photograph, pulled it out and began rubbing it like a crucifix.

What you got there, Russell? the doctor said. You're not looking so good.

It's a picture of a girl, I said. Alana is her name. She's missing. She's in danger.

Sure, sure, the sheriff said. We know all about her. Alana. Yes, sir. I've got my men looking into her disappearance right now. No need for you to worry.

Factory Town

We'll find her, you can be sure about that...

And that's when I heard screams coming from the hallway. The men looked at each other; didn't do anything but raise their eyebrows and shake their heads. The shrieking continued.

What the hell is going on? I said.

Nothing, the pastor said. You stay right here with us. You don't worry about that screaming. Just a girl having a good time is all. A town of debauchery, I tell you.

I stood there for a moment, thinking. Then I rushed toward the door.

CHAPTER 5

The hallway was now crowded with people, but they were all quiet, leaning against the wall, eyes all gazing in the same direction. The screaming was unmistakably that of a woman, but it was that of agony, not ecstasy. Nobody in the hallway made any motion to investigate the commotion and, in fact, as I hurried down the hallway, they turned to each other and shook their heads and murmured their disapproval. When I glanced back, I could see the sheriff and his cronies standing outside of the cards room, hands on hips or arms folded, watching dispassionately, making no move to assist.

And then the screaming stopped. Suddenly and completely. I slowed down my pace but continued walking, determined to find the woman in distress. The sudden quiet was disconcerting and caused me worry. Had she been hurt badly enough to silence her

Factory Town

voice? I turned back around. The throngs of people who had been crowded against the walls had now vanished, disappeared to the lower floor or into one of the bedrooms. It was just me. As I edged forward, out of the corner of my eye, I noticed a photograph hanging from the wall. A young boy, seven or eight years old, face contorted into a scowl. Behind the boy, a metal swing set and green grass forever, forever. And the boy in the picture was me.

I couldn't remember when or where the photograph was taken, but I remembered the photograph itself. My eyes scanned the walls and I saw other photographs, photographs of me, photographs of my family. And then I tilted my head back and gazed at the ceiling and saw the familiar floral tile pattern, and for the first time I realized that I was in the house of my childhood. I had not recognized the house because it was in such disrepair, but now things were clearer and memories started flooding back. The hours playing with my prized superhero action figures, climbing up walls, destroying the evil around us. Or sitting in the corner of my room, writing adventure stories, illustrating them with stubs of colored pencils. Reading my prized comics: Spiderman and Batman and Superman and The Fantastic Four and… So many hours alone. Because my mother was sick. Because my father… My thoughts were interrupted by more screaming.

They were coming from the room directly in front of me. Louder than ever. And in between the screams and gasps, cries of help me, help me. I tried twisting the knob but it was locked, so I pounded on the door again and again, until my hands were raw. No answer, only more screaming. This much was clear: nobody would help this woman, nobody but me. They'd just as soon let her die. I started kicking, but the door was heavy and didn't budge. I felt helpless. I kicked some more, pounded some more, shouted, Are you okay in there? Hang in there, you hear me?

Time passed and my voice was hoarse and my hands were bleeding and the screaming continued. They'd let her die. That's the way things were in Factory Town.

One more kick and the door flew open, slamming against the interior wall. Breathing hard, I stepped inside the room, badly cluttered with clothes and bottles and prescription vials. There was splintered furniture covered with music boxes and magazines, and antique dolls staring at me with dead eyes. On the walls, paintings of desert landscapes and a Thomas Kincaid calendar from long ago. The window was open and the white curtain was whipping around in a great panic.

On the bed was a man with enormous girth, belly bulging, thinning black hair combed back into an attempted pompadour, face red with exertion. And beneath him, a woman, wearing nothing but winter socks, her face bleeding badly, her nose busted beyond repair, eyes as dead as her antique dolls.

She was in bad shape and she was moaning and crying and the man was fucking her and punching her and strangling her, and she was bound to die if I didn't step in and help, if I didn't pull the man off of her body, but I was suddenly paralyzed, couldn't move at all. Somehow, neither of them had noticed my presence. I tried calling out but could produce no

Factory Town

sound other than a strange guttural noise, one that blended in to the moaning and crying and shouting. My muscles had somehow atrophied, and eventually I collapsed to the floor. The man turned the woman over and pushed her face into the pillow. Her back was covered with an enormous tattoo: a magnificent phoenix rising from the ashes, the sun burning brightly behind it. The woman was struggling for air, her arms thrashing wildly, and then he reached over to the nightstand and grabbed his lit cigarette and pressed it against the skin on her lower back. Her back arched in pain, but the man shoved her down, gave her another three or four burns before crushing out the cigarette on the wall and tossing it to the ground.

I was lying on my stomach, my legs all withered away, and in the manner of a wounded soldier I tried pulling myself forward with my arms, but the going was slow. The man sat up in bed, slicked back his hair with a palm-full of Dixie Peach hair pomade, and then placed a tattered cowboy's hat on his head. He grabbed a bottle of vodka by the neck and swallowed down his fair share, his Adam's apple bobbing up and down. The woman curled up into a fetal position, the pillow smeared with her blood and tears.

For a long time they stayed like that, him sitting at the side of the bed drinking vodka and smoking cigarettes, her coiled on top of the blankets, face starting to swell badly.

After a while he spoke, and his voice was deep and full of gravel. Don't like doing that, he said, but sometimes I don't have no choice.

No answer from the woman, just sobbing.

Jon Bassoff

He tipped up his cowboy's hat and nodded. Ed told me you was getting friendly with that boy from the filling station. Said you let him have a feel and a kiss. You're my wife, damn it, you made certain pledges, certain promises. I don't like hurting you. But there ain't no place for whores in this here house. Whores get beat. That's only fair.

And then the man rose from the bed and wandered across the room to where a sink was. He turned on the faucet and started scrubbing his hands with a bar of black soap. He scrubbed and he scrubbed until I could see his hands becoming red and raw. This goddamn town, he said. Goddamn factory. Can't ever get the stink from my hands...

Meanwhile, I was still on the ground desperately trying to pull myself forward, but now my arms and spine were also going numb, a rotten situation.

It's all them chemicals spewing from the factory, the man said. That must be what causes all the insanity and all the awful things that I do. But I never mean to hurt you. You believe me, Nicole, don't you? You forgive me, don't you?

The woman, Nicole, straightened her body and rolled on her back. Her face was a pulpy mess, with the blood and the bruises and the swelling. I forgive you, she said, barely louder than a whisper. Sure, I forgive you. You got mad. We all get mad. But listen to me, Cory Packer. I never fooled around with that boy. I've always been true. If Ed told you otherwise then he's a liar.

Cory shook his head. Don't surprise me. Ed, he ain't nothing but a good ol' boy. He makes up stories. I shouldn't have listened to him.

Factory Town

I never fooled around with that boy, she said again.

Cory walked across the room, stepping over my outstretched arms, and sat back on the bed. He pulled his wife to a sitting position and then he held her, stroking her dishwater blonde hair and kissing her battered forehead. I ain't gonna do it again, he said. I ain't gonna hit you again. Never, ever. You understand that? You believe that?

They sat like that for a long time, and everything was quiet, and the curtains were swaying, and if you overlooked the blood and bruising and swelling that the man had inflicted upon his wife, they looked the part of domestic tranquility.

And then my body spasmed back to life, the paralysis over. I got to my hands and knees and started to crawl toward the door. I didn't notice, however, a broken beer bottle on the floor, and as I moved forward, a shard of glass lodged in the palm of my hand. I gasped in pain. Cory sat up, said, Who the hell is that? Boy, is that you? You in here spying again, you little snot-nosed punk?

In a great state of panic, I dropped to my stomach, rolled under the bed, and held my breath.

Cory rose from bed, and I watched as he paced back and forth across the floor. Where are you, boy? I know you're in here. Come on out so I can kick the goddamn shit out of you! Cursing, he ripped back the curtain and slammed open the closet door and, finally, got down on his hands and knees and peered under the bed, face red and angry, but I had hidden myself well, in the corner, under layers of moth-eaten blankets.

Jon Bassoff

Nicole's voice: Please, Cory. Leave him alone. He hasn't done nothing.

The hell he hasn't! We all done something! We're all sinners in the eyes of the Lord! We're all sinners in the eyes of me! Come on out, boy! Where you hiding? I know you're in here somewhere. Come on out so I can show you what I really think of you! You little freak! Wearing that goddamn cape every day. And that goddamn mask. Who you think you gonna save? Huh? Who you think you gonna save? Piece of shit. Piece of miserable shit.

But after a while, he got tired of searching the room and crawled back into the bed, the mattress sagging beneath his enormous mass. Then he started laughing, loud and mean.

What's so funny? Nicole said. Why are you laughing?

Just a joke I heard once, he said.

I stayed under the bed for a long time, hours maybe, until finally I heard the old man snoring, dead to the world. I crawled out from beneath the bed and rose to my feet, head foggy and hands trembling.

The man, Cory, was sound asleep, eyes rolled back into his head, jaw slack, but his wife, Nicole, was still awake. Our eyes met, and her mouth opened as if she was going to say something, but then she just shook her head and closed her eyes. Her hand softly rubbed her belly, a slight bulge there. Feeling good and sick, I walked out of the room, shutting the door gently behind me.

CHAPTER 6

I walked through the hallway of my childhood house and down the staircase. The band had stopped playing and the party was slowing down. On a corner couch, an old man with a porkpie hat and three fingers on his right hand drank a mint julep, while a young woman with bubblegum pink hair and an argyle sweater sat on his lap. A woman with insane eyes magnified through Coke-bottle glasses sat on the floor mourning the loss of something. A businessman with his toupee askew paced the floor searching for his dignity and his car keys. A couple of identical Hispanic girls were leaning against the wall, whispering and giggling behind their hands. And Charlie Gardner, my childhood friend, was standing in the middle of the floor, lips spread in a wide grin. Well, there you are, buddy boy, he said. I was beginning to worry about you. Everything okay with that woman? That fellow Corey Packer is one mean bastard, isn't he? I would have liked to have helped you back there, but you know how things are. Well, what you say we head back to my place and get some shuteye? You gotta be well-rested if you're gonna find that missing girl, don't you think?

I couldn't argue with him. As we walked out the door, the band started playing again and it was *Love Me Tender* and Elvis was dead.

* * *

The night had gotten colder and the snow was falling, whipped around by gusts of wind. We walked in silence, our shoes crunching on the dirt and snow. When I glanced back, I saw that the house was dark. The party was over. I wondered if the woman, Nicole, was okay. A man hits you once, he'll hit you again.

I don't live far away, Charlie said, and we continued walking.

We walked through the neighborhood of ranch houses and chain link fences. Ghostly faces peered out from behind foggy windows, the occasional blue light of a television flickering behind them. And a few windows were open, and I could hear furtive whisperings and murmurs. The air was cold, and my lungs burned.

We walked for some time, and the moon vanished behind a blackened cloud. Up ahead, in an open field, the headlights of a long American car shone, illuminating an old man in a pea coat and red scarf digging a hole with a shovel. There was no one else around.

What's this guy doing? I said.

Factory Town

Charlie grabbed my arm. Leave it alone. Best mind your own business in this town.

But I was hearing that sentiment too much. Ignoring Charlie, I walked toward the glare of the headlights, stood next to the car, which was still running, humming softly. The old man looked up, his face ashen, his gray hair splayed wildly. For a while we just stared at each other, his blue eyes shining like a feral cat. Then he looked back down and continued digging. And as he dug, it occurred to me that I knew this man, that I knew everybody in this town, though I'd never been here, though I was a stranger, only searching for the girl, my lovely Alana.

He was old and feeble and was having great difficulty digging through the frozen ground. I took a few steps forward. The old man grunted, pointed at another shovel lying on the ground, said, Watcha waiting for, boy? I could sure use some help.

He bent down and picked up the second shovel, tossed it at my feet. The blade was dull and rusted, the handle splintered. I picked it up. My brain felt sick, vile thoughts crawling around like cockroaches.

I didn't ask questions, just started digging. The old man didn't help. He leaned against the hood of his car and greedily sucked a cigarette. Charlie, what had happened to Charlie? It didn't matter. I worked hard, jamming the blade into the frigid ground, tossing the dirt aside. I don't know why. Faster and faster I worked while the old man watched and the moon reappeared then shattered into a million pieces, scattered around my feet.

He ain't here yet, the old man said, but it's only a matter of time. Just need some mortician's wax to fill the wound.

I didn't look up, just kept digging.

Shot himself with a pistol. Stuck the barrel to his temple and fired. 3200 feet per second. Past hair, skin and muscle. Gun smoke and powder burning his flesh. Shrapnel in his skull.

The wind was whipping angrily and I could hear a murder of crows roosting in a nearby tree. My muscles were aching and I was sweating despite the cold.

But I guess he's lucky. If he'd shot himself in the heart it would've taken some time. Could've uttered last words, spent some time thinking about his predicament. But not this fellow. Just a fragment of a second. An explosion of nerve cells and synapses. A lifetime of memories splattered on the hardwood floor.

One thing was certain: The man was eccentric, crazy maybe. I didn't respond to his ramblings.

It was backbreaking work, digging this hole. Time passed, an hour or more, and I'd barely made a dent, maybe gotten two feet down, two feet wide. I looked up at the old man. He was nibbling from a bottle of bourbon, a crooked grin on his face. Keep going, he said. You're doing a hell of a job.

I shook my head in disgust, spat on the dirt. The ground is too hard, I said. We need to wait until it warms up some.

Can't afford to wait. Gotta have a grave to put him in. Gotta show a little respect. Don't want the Vultures to get him.

I jammed my shovel in the ground, left it upright. I'm sorry, but I can't help you anymore. I've gotta get some rest. I'm in the midst of an important investigation. You see, I'm looking for this girl and her name—

Factory Town

The old man interrupted me. I know about the girl. Everybody knows about the girl.

But how...

You should see Miguel Romero. Some people say he can heal the sick. Some people say he can raise the dead. Some people say he's the Messiah. Surely he can find the little girl for you. Surely...

At that moment, Charlie appeared from behind a tree. In his right hand he held an enormous crow, good and dead. He tossed it toward the old man, said, You can bury this bird in the meantime. The poor thing musta ate itself to death.

The old man picked up the bird and studied it. Strange things are happening, he said. It's because of the factory. All them chemicals leaking into the town's hippocampus...

*   *   *

Charlie and I kept walking, but his house wasn't close like he'd said. Three miles, maybe more, but it was hard to say because it seemed like we were walking in circles; I kept seeing the same run-down houses and wrecked cars, the same nightmare trees, branches gnarled and crooked. Charlie walked quickly, and I had a hard time keeping up with him.

As we walked through the cold night, I pulled out the photograph and studied it again compulsively, looking for a clue or for inspiration, anything that would push me closer to learning her whereabouts. The man. I gazed at the man, barely visible. An overwhelming feeling of familiarity spread through my consciousness. I knew this man, I was sure of it.

Jon Bassoff

But how? Had I seen him in Factory Town, in passing maybe, a stranger whose eyes met mine for a moment before ducking into some filthy alley? The problem was my senses, my memory. I couldn't trust them; lack of sleep had made them unreliable, prone to illusion...

I heard Charlie's voice, calling out to me. He was up ahead a ways, leaning against an ancient oak tree, blowing into a harmonica, playing an old blues song I'd heard in another life:

My girl, my girl, where will you go
I'm going where the cold wind blows
In the pines, in the pines
Where the sun don't ever shine
I would shiver the whole night through

* * *

I stood next to him, puffing tendrils of frigid air. He stuck the harmonica into his pocket and grinned. We're almost there, he said. I miscalculated how long it would take. You doing okay there, buddy boy?

I'm doing fine, I said, but we've been walking a long time. Do you mind if we sit, just for a minute?

Not at all.

We sat down beneath the oak tree, and somewhere in the distance I heard a train whistle blowing, all twisted from the wind, and suddenly I felt scared, overwhelmingly so, but of what, but of who?

Charlie pulled out a bag of leaf chewing tobacco and offered me a dip. I refused and he shrugged and then stuck a big wad in between his right cheek and

Factory Town

lower gum. He spat a stream of brown juice on the ground and wiped his mouth with his forearm. In the faint light of the moon, his face looked gaunt, sunken, bleach white.

And this town, this land, he said, is a place of darkness.

It was a strange thing to say, uttered without context, but I accepted his comment in silence.

He continued: My mother, she's very sick. She doesn't have long to live. Still, she'd like to see you.

Yes, I said. I'd like to see her, too.

You won't recognize her, I'm afraid. She's stopped eating. It's her way of revenge, I suppose.

I felt a wave of exhaustion, physically, emotionally, mentally, and I closed my eyes. I just needed some sleep, a small respite, then I could continue the investigation. I slumped down on the cold ground, using a rock for a pillow and the wind for my blanket. I began drifting, drifting, feeling the sweet numbness of slumber enveloping my body...

Charlie shook my shoulders. C'mon fellow, he said, don't give up now. My house is just up ahead.

My eyes opened but I didn't speak; I was too tired to say another word.

It's right there, he said, pointing straight ahead. I pulled myself to a sitting position and stared in the direction he was pointing. Indeed, less than a hundred yards away, there was a small house, a shack really, nestled in a crown of trees.

And just beyond the shack, I could see the white farmhouse from which we'd just come.

CHAPTER 7

The inside of the shack was strange. The floors were covered with green felt, and the chairs were all mismatched, Mexican style. On the walls were photographs of insects: jewel beetles, peacock swallowtails, dobsonflies. And in the corner of the room, in a large aquarium, a snapping turtle, its skin a sickly yellow.

Get you something to drink, pal? Charlie asked, his smile as wide as ever.

I shook my head. No, thanks. I just need to sleep.

Sure, sure, I understand. Like I said, you'll be sharing a room with my mother. She's very sick. Stopped eating. But don't worry, she won't bother you. She just sleeps all day, hardly moves. You won't hardly recognize her, Russell. It's a shame, don't you think? God can be cruel.

Factory Town

He showed me where the bathroom was, handed me a beach towel in case I needed to shower, then took me to his mother's room. It was small: more like a closet than a bedroom, but each of the walls was mirrored, making the room seem infinite. There were no windows, of course, and no furniture other than the single bed in the middle of the room, covered with a heap of blankets, Charlie's diseased mother hidden beneath.

Well, this is it, he said. It's not much, I know, but at least you'll have a place to lay your head...

I shook my head. Well, it's fine, I said, only it doesn't look like there is any place for me to sleep. I mean, there's only one bed.

Charlie smiled. No need to be modest, buddy. You can share it with my mother. She won't bother you. She won't even move, I bet.

Charlie, I don't know...

It would mean a lot to her, Russell. Just to have a warm body next to her. She doesn't have long to live, you know.

I sighed and nodded my head. I was too tired to argue. Okay, I said. Okay.

Thanks, buddy. You'll sleep like a log. It's a waterbed. You like waterbeds?

Yeah, sure...

That's great, buddy. And then tomorrow, you'll be well rested and you can continue your investigation. Alana is her name, right? Yes, yes, we'll find her. I'm sure it's all just a misunderstanding. I'm sure she's safe. There's a guy you should talk to. He's the Messiah. No kidding. He'll know where she is.

And then Charlie was gone, and I stood in the

middle of the room, the mirrors causing my reflection to repeat forever. Head spinning, eyes heavy, I managed to stumble to the bed and lie down, still fully clothed. The mattress swayed, but Charlie's mother, buried under the blankets, didn't stir. There wasn't much room on the bed, hardly any at all. I lay on my back, on top of the sheets and blankets, my left arm and left leg dangling over the side of the bed. My body started to relax, just for a moment. Then I realized the lights were still on, bright fluorescent lights. I sighed deeply. I pulled myself out of bed and staggered across the room, but I couldn't find the light switch anywhere.

This wouldn't do. I needed to sleep, but I couldn't do so with the bright lights glaring overhead. I would ask Charlie for assistance. Perhaps the light switch was outside the room. But finding the door proved to be an equally difficult task, the mirrors causing the room to expand and condense, expand and condense. I got frustrated, overwhelmed. It must have been a pathetic sight, me crashing against the walls like a trapped moth, pulling out my hair like a madman. Forgetting the diseased woman lying motionless in the waterbed, I began shouting out for Charlie, pounding on the mirrored walls, my face bug-eyed and panicked, until one of them finally shattered, shards everywhere, causing my hands to bloody. I spotted the door behind the splintered glass, so I stepped out of the room, still calling for Charlie, my childhood friend, but he was nowhere to be found. I wandered to the living area. The front door was wide open, the snow was blowing into the shack, and Charlie had vanished.

Factory Town

Back in the mirrored room, still brightly lit, now freezing cold, and I returned to the bed and burrowed under the covers, shivering badly. I could feel her body, cold, dead perhaps, and I squeezed my eyes shut, trying to will sleep to come, but my mind was deteriorating due to the fumes from the factory...

For hours I lay in bed, next to this strange woman, and she didn't move, didn't move at all. And just when I'd decided to get out of bed and break out of this strange little house, just when I'd decided that this insomnia was an incurable disease, I felt her move, felt her touch my arm, and I gasped.

She pulled the covers down slowly, and, in fear, I toppled out of bed and came crashing to the hardwood floor. I sat on my haunches, heart beating rapidly. Wheezing heavily, she managed to pull herself to an upright position and then sat there leaning against the headboard, staring at me behind black eyes sunken in yellowed skin. Her face was that of a skeleton, her body that of a corpse. Her hair was steely gray.

After a few moments, she turned her gaze toward the shattered mirror, her reflection a Picasso painting. Then she reached across to the nightstand and grabbed a brush. With long, sweeping motions she began brushing her hair. I watched her from the floor, with that familiar feeling of dread. And as she brushed, I noticed that the hair was falling out in clumps.

You must be one of Charlie's friends, she said.

Yes. I didn't mean to intrude. I only needed a place to sleep and he said I could—

Did he tell you that I was sick?

I nodded my head. Yes, he did.

Well, he's wrong. I'm not sick. It's my husband. He's a wicked person. He's paranoid. So he beats me. He poisons me. He caused a miscarriage. I've had enough. I'm ready to die. So I've stopped eating. It's the best way, really. Look at me. I'm just a skeleton. Not much more.

I shook my head in disbelief. You're talking about Charlie's father? But he's such a well-respected member of society. Hardly an ill word spoken about him. I have a hard time believing he'd do those things.

But it's true. He's a monster. A tormenter. Don't let his charming exterior fool you. If you had an ounce of mercy you would slit his throat. I would be ever so thankful. I could repay you somehow. I am still a woman after all.

That's crazy, I said. I've never even—

It wouldn't be difficult. They'd never suspect you...

No. I'm not killing anybody. I'm a protector, not a killer.

What's the matter? she said. Don't you care about me, Russell? Don't you think I'm pretty?

I was taken off guard. I nodded my head slowly. I studied her face, her eyes, trying to recall, just trying to recall. She *had* once been beautiful, so beautiful that I almost believed in God, but beauty falls apart, just like everything, rusts and rots, disintegrates and deteriorates. Skin peels back and reveals bleach-white bones, nothing more, and all of our laughter is buried beneath the dirt, listen closely. Yes, I said. I think you're pretty. Of course I do.

She gazed at me for a long time and a sad smile

Factory Town

spread across her face. I know you're lying, of course I do. But sometimes lies can be the kindest words of all, don't you think?

And then the tears came. She tried shielding her face from me, but the walls were all mirrored and there was no hiding. I placed my arms around her wasted body and said, Don't cry, ma'am, please don't cry. Not now. Not yet.

I can't help it, she said. I hurt all over.

And so we lay there together, and I could feel the rats eating worms from my skull, and she was wasting away, a protest against the world.

Why don't you leave? I finally whispered. Get out of Factory Town.

No. It's too late. Where would I go?

It doesn't matter. Anywhere but here. Somewhere far away.

Charlie's mother wiped a tear from her cheek and smiled a sad smile. I can't leave, she said. You know that. Nobody can leave.

What are you talking about?

The guards. They protect the perimeter of Factory Town. And they'll shoot down anybody who tries to leave.

I shook my head. I think you're mistaken. I just arrived here. I didn't see any guards. I'm sure I would have noticed.

The guards are there. Everybody says so. And besides—she pulled down the covers below her knees—my husband has seen to it that I'll never leave this town.

I gazed down in disbelief. The bile rose in my throat. Both her legs ended in grotesque stumps, the

Jon Bassoff

result of a saw or a hatchet.

Jesus Christ. He did this?

She nodded her head. So I couldn't run.

I can save you, I said. Maybe that's what I'm here for. By killing him, huh? Just by killing him? Maybe I could. Maybe...

Charlie's mother thought things over for a few moments. Then she shook her head. No, Russell. I shouldn't have said anything. You don't have it in you. I can see that now. And that's a good thing. He's a monster. You're something better. You're not like him. So just leave me be. That's the best thing you can do. Factory Town isn't forever.

I shook my head. I could save you both. If I just believe. If I just believe hard enough.

Stop. Please. It's too late for that.

But—

No. Leave me be. And leave her be, too.

There was no use arguing with her. I lay back on the bed and closed my eyes, heavy with exhaustion. I fell asleep for no more than a minute; the digital clock, stuck on 11:57, didn't change. But when I opened my eyes the old woman was gone.

I gritted my teeth and clenched my fists. This goddamn town, I whispered. Then, instinctively, I touched my temple with my fingers before bringing them in front of my eyes.

They were covered with fresh blood.

CHAPTER 8

Mrs. Gardner had said the world would be a better place without her husband. But I knew better.

The world would only be a better place without every damn one of us.

Outside, and the sun and moon were both hanging low in the sky. The air was cold and everything smelled like smoke. I started walking and, in addition to the wound on my temple, felt a dull ache in my stomach. Other than my forced feeding of raw ostrich meat, I hadn't had a bite to eat since my arrival.

I wandered through the neighborhoods, uncertain of which direction to walk, searching for the factory smokestacks to guide me back to town. Abandoned houses, junkyard cars. Not a soul in sight.

I buried my hands in my pocket and walked along the yellowed sidewalk, weeds and brown grass pushing through the cracks. And then I heard the

Jon Bassoff

sounds of footsteps behind me. Whipping my head around, I spotted the figure of a man, gaining ground quickly. He had silver hair slicked straight back and wore a white suit, all spattered with red mud. And now he was waving his arms frantically, trying to get my attention, but I ignored him, continued walking. I couldn't have any more distractions, any more interruptions. I needed to find my way back to town, get some food, maybe some sleep, and then continue my search.

And so I quickened my pace, but then he took up a full sprint, shouting out, Russell Carver, I need to speak to you! Russell Carver! I stopped and turned, waited for the strange man to catch up.

His face was red and bloated, broken capillaries covering his cheeks, and he was wheezing badly. In his right hand he clutched a thick book, the cover leather and worn.

Russell Carver, he said again. I've been searching for you. Since your arrival. They wanted me to talk to you. I felt it was unnecessary. But they insisted. You are not an easy man to find, Russell Carver. I figured you'd be in the factory, earning a living like the rest of us. But you never showed up. You never clocked in. I should know. I stood there by the timecards all day yesterday. But you never came. Yes, indeed, you are a hard man to find!

I was shaken by his rambling. Who are you? I said.

Yes, yes. Terribly sorry. How rude of me. Michael Fennington. I work for the Cowboy. His secretary of sorts, I guess you could say.

The Cowboy?

Factory Town

Certainly.

I'm sorry, I said, but I don't know who the Cowboy is. That is, I've heard his name mentioned but...

Fennington looked at me with a bemused expression. Then he nodded his head. Of course, he said. I forget that you are only a visitor. I forget that you don't know the ins and outs of Factory Town. We don't have a traditional municipality here. No mayor. No court system. No jails. You see, Mr. Carver, we have our own way of dealing with problems, our own way of dealing with troublemakers. And the Cowboy, he oversees the entire operation. A great deal of respect he has earned for his leadership. Bringing various factions together at the bargaining table. Searching for common ground while holding steadfast to his principles. A true visionary. A true American. In fact, it was he who authored the *Book of Edicts*.

The *Book of Edicts*?

Yes, sir. And it might do you some good to read it. To help you understand.

I felt my irritation, my frustration beginning to boil. I don't have time to read your laws, I said. I have important business here; that is finding the girl, Alana.

Yes, yes, of course. Alana. So sad that she's gone missing. And that's what I wanted to talk to you about. Exactly what I wanted to talk to you about.

We were now standing face to face, the trees swaying menacingly, the sky gunmetal gray.

Okay, I said. Talk.

But perhaps in a different setting? Perhaps in my car? I could give you a ride back to town. You seem to have lost your way.

Jon Bassoff

I thought things over for a minute. Fine, I said. I could certainly use a lift.

He led me away from the sidewalk and down a dirt alleyway where his car was parked, an old '58 Packard, jet black. He opened the passenger side door for me, gestured with his hand, and I slid inside, the seats white vinyl. Then he got in the car, slicked back his hair with his palm, and hit the engine.

And so we drove. The music played softly, Bing Crosby, and Fennington puffed on a Fatima cigarette. I rolled down the window, despite the cold, trying to breathe in fresh air. There were no other cars driving on the street, although there were quite a few of them abandoned on the side of the road, a few of them on fire.

Miles and miles of asphalt, and Fennington's leathery face became more and more brooding. When Fennington spoke, his voice was barely louder than a whisper. The Cowboy, he said, is very interested in you.

Interested in me?

Indeed. He thinks you can be of great help in finding the girl, Alana. Yes, he's quite interested in her safe return.

But the way he said it gave me chills. I breathed deeply, gripped the seat cushion. What does the Cowboy care about the girl for? I asked.

Oh, he cares about every little girl and every little boy in town. A kind-hearted man is he. But more importantly, he has a great interest in lawfulness and order. Her disappearance has caused great agitation.

At this, I shrugged my shoulders. Unfortunately, I said, I can't help you. I've been looking, but I don't

Factory Town

know where she is. And nobody in this town seems willing or able to help.

Yes, yes. I share your frustrations. We don't have many leads ourselves. But the Cowboy wanted me to reach out to you, wanted to make sure we are all on the same page. United we stand and so forth.

I understand.

No, he said, I don't think you do. Her safe recovery is crucial for the future of Factory Town. If we can't find her, then...

He stopped talking and reached into his jacket pocket. He pulled out a stack of green, secured by a black rubber band. He tossed it on my lap.

What the hell is this?

Five thousand dollars, he said.

I picked it up, but didn't say anything.

Keep the money. Buy yourself something nice. Some new clothes. A new whore. Meanwhile, keep looking for the girl. When you find her, bring her to me. I'm staying at the Lullaby Motel, right across from the abandoned drive-in theatre. Then you'll get ten more. Tax free, of course.

This doesn't make any sense. This...

Suddenly, he stopped the car. He said: I'm afraid this is as far as I can take you. You need to get out now. We were in the middle of nowhere, wheat fields swaying all around.

You said you would take me back to town.

I'm sorry, but we can't be seen together. You'll find your way. I have great confidence in you, Russell. The Cowboy has great confidence in you.

* * *

Jon Bassoff

And so I staggered through the wheat fields and I had five thousand dollars and a picture of a girl, not much else. Everything was wrong. My temple was throbbing. I touched the skin; the wound had reopened and my fingers were once again bloody. I needed to see a doctor or maybe a mortician...

The weather changed quickly. Lightning flashed from every direction, illuminating the sky, and the rain fell in torrents, sheets and sheets crashing to the ground. A thousand crows flew across the sky, the next great plague. And somewhere in the distance, buried beneath the soaked dirt, the sound of muffled screaming, the dead having their way with the living.

And then the lightning ceased and the rain turned to snow. At first it was soft and slow and brought memories of childhood, but then the gods decided to teach me a lesson or two, and it turned into a blizzard, visibility gone quickly. Only a few minutes and the snow was nearly up to my knees. I could barely walk. I breathed deeply, felt the coldness on my skin, the coldness in my soul, and I was miles from town, miles from my childhood home, miles from my wife, my wife, my wife...

Eventually, I could go no farther. The snow began turning red, and I fell to my knees, and then to my face, and then all I heard was strange gypsy music.

* * *

And so it was that I somehow lived, carried through the snow drifts by an immense man who

Factory Town

was unable or unwilling to speak, and dropped in the care of Sister Patricia who lived in a tin shack overlooking Factory Town. It was she who nursed me back to health, her face blurry at first, but gradually becoming clearer, the face of an angel despite the scars around her eyes.

The room was stark: only the bed in the middle of the floor, only a cross in the middle of the wall. A single window, the curtains drawn. I tried pushing off the covers, tried rising from the bed, but Sister Patricia wouldn't allow it, saying, You need rest, my dear. You've been badly wounded, don't you see?

And so she cleaned out my wound with boric acid, gave me water from a bucket, and fed me crackers, the first food I'd eaten in days. She didn't press me to talk, didn't ask how I'd ended up in the wheat field, but I felt compelled to anyway. There was this man, I said. He called himself Fennington. He wore a white hat and a white suit, filthy with what I now believe was blood. He said he represented somebody named the Cowboy. He talked about law and justice. He talked about the *Book of Edicts*. And when I mentioned the girl, Alana, he was greatly interested, although his interest seemed more predatory than protective. He gave me five thousand dollars and promised more once I find her.

At this, the nun's brow furrowed and her eyes narrowed. You're right to be suspicious, she said. The Cowboy is a bad man, an evil man. Everybody knows it. But nobody will do anything about it.

Why is he bad? What has he done? What is his interest in Alana?

Sister Patricia stared at me for a long moment

and then turned away. She rose from her chair and walked over to the window, stood there wringing her hands. You're being set up, she said quietly. Made to be the fool.

Set up?

It's a terrible place, Factory Town. And the Cowboy and his crew, they're more terrible than most. They'll take what they can and, once they're done, they'll do some terrible things. Believe me, sir, believe me.

And then the nun told me a story about Factory Town, and I believed every word because I chose to, we chose to.

This land has always been harsh and cruel, the nun said, no good for farming, no good for settling. In the beginning, near the turn of the century, it was called Homestead, and it wasn't anything but a little railroad town, a shipping point with the Northern Pacific. There weren't but a handful of residents and most of them worked for the railroad. Then, in 1910 or thereabouts, the state decided to open up a psychiatric hospital right outside of town. They called it Warm Springs Asylum, and even changed the name of the town to Warm Springs, even though there wasn't a single spring in the area. I guess they figured that a stark, rural setting would do the sick minds some good. And this hospital didn't house your typical manic-depressives or dementia patients either. No, sir, Warm Springs was filled with the criminally insane, lunatics who had drowned their children or skinned their husbands or plucked the eyes from their bosses. Demonic stuff, you understand.

The nun took a few steps forward, her expression

Factory Town

somber. Move ahead a decade or so, she said. A businessman named Dominic Farley moved to Montana and decided to open up a sugar beet factory in town, less than a mile from the asylum. The town grew a bit, jobs were to be had. But Farley wasn't making the kind of money he wanted or expected to make. Then he had some sort of a revelation. He had read about Australia and how that country got built. Free labor. You know the story. The English got rid of their criminals, sent them to Australia to help build the country. It worked out okay, down under, why not here?

He met with the leaders of the hospital. Here was a win-win situation. Allow the hospital to reduce its overcrowding by allowing some of its rehabilitated convicts into a work-release program. Free labor initially, and if they proved themselves to be competent, then soon they would be paid competitive wages.

So they started working. A bunch of crazy folks doing plant maintenance, moving finished sugar from the warehouse, stockpiling coal and limestone brought in by the railroad, and so on and so on.

But Mr. Farley was a bastard and a cheapskate. He never planned on paying the workers a dime, even after they proved their worth. So that's when the real trouble began. They started to rebel. They started destroying the factory. Farley tried calling in hospital security, tried calling in the proper authorities, but it was too late. Chaos ensued. The insane did what they knew how to do. They butchered each other, they butchered the supervisors. Tormenting screams mixed with lunatic laughter. Heads and arms and legs chopped off. They impaled poor Dominic Farley with a metal pole and threw him into one of the centrifugal machines. Pretty soon the factory was filled with nothing but blood and corpses. Most of the survivors fled. A handful of lunatics remained. And they lived. And they bred.

The nun looked down and her eyes were too pained to cry.

I shook my head. But I still don't understand. What does the history of Factory Town have to do with anything?

A legacy of sin, she said. Hell on Earth. A town in need of death.

What are you saying? I still don't—

Surely you've noticed...

Noticed what?

That there are no children in this town. No children at all.

I thought for a moment. It was true. That was a part of the strangeness. No children at all. But then I remembered the boy from the building. The Annihilator.

There was one boy, I said. In the basement of the hotel.

Sister Patricia stood next to me and shook her head. Listen good, Mr. Carver. Forget what you think you may have seen. There are no children in this town.

But—

Do you hear me? There are no children in this town.

CHAPTER 9

Sister Patricia left me alone, staring at the cross, wondering at the possibilities of my own resurrection, bloody as they may be. I rose from bed and walked over to the window, pulled back the curtains and gazed at the living ghost town below. Such dreariness. Such misery. A town in need of death. But who would be willing to strangle away its last breath, killing himself in the process?

I staggered down the hallway to the bathroom. I pissed in the toilet, vomited in the sink. Then I stared at my face. She'd bandaged the wound, but blood was beginning to seep through. My eyes were bloodshot and darting across my skull like fingerlings. *Why wouldn't they be scared of you?* the Annihilator had said. *Why wouldn't they? You do terrible things. You're just like my father. You even look like him. You have the same eyes.* I slammed my fist against the mirror but it did no good, wouldn't shatter. Then I sat down on the commode and cried, tears of regret burning my eyes like cyanide.

I pulled out the photograph of Alana and studied it for a good long time. The photograph was changing again, not my sick mind, not my sick mind. The figure of the man was becoming clearer: broad shoulders, flannel shirt, carpenter jeans. Only his face was still hazy, undetermined.

I returned to the bedroom and got dressed as the curtains swayed in the breeze. I needed to leave. I needed to continue my investigation. I needed to find the girl, before she died, before I died. And not for the Cowboy's blood money. I would throw that money off the back of a train; I would bury that money in the wheat fields; I would gift it to the wind.

But when I reached for the stack of hundreds in the nightstand drawer there was nothing but a note written in the voluminous handwriting of the nun: Money taken for services rendered.

The nun had taken me for all I was worth.

* * *

Back outside and I felt hazy and hungry and exhausted. I couldn't sleep, but I couldn't wake. I wondered if anybody missed me. Heartache was nothing new, but pity I don't ask for.

It was dusk or dawn; the differences didn't matter. The streets were empty; the town was quiet. Everything was covered with snow, filthy always. As I walked through town, I realized that I'd misplaced my jacket and my flannel. I wore only jeans and a

Factory Town

Popeye T-shirt, not enough for the snow and cold. My head was down and I was mumbling to myself, something I did from time to time. I replayed the facts of the case. The warnings from the whore: *You ain't gonna find nothing here. You ain't gonna find that girl.* The Annihilator and his secret world. The apathy and callousness of the townsfolk. The Cowboy and his predatory interest in Alana, his *Book of Edicts*.

Still, I was no closer to finding Alana; in fact, I felt as lost and alone as ever. And then, as I continued trudging through the snow, something caught my eye. A large piece of paper, elaborately designed, taped to a broken window. It was a poster, designed like one of those old circus advertisements, with yellow and orange stripes alternating vertically down the paper. In the middle of the page was a picture of a man with a shaved head and a long beard, wearing a tunic, placing his hand on the eyes of a young woman. On the top of the poster, in cartoon letters: HUNTER TIMILLI PREZENTS THE MESIAH. And then at the bottom, in smaller letters: YOU MUST BELEVE!!! GOD HAS RETURND ONCE AGEN TO RELEVE US OF OUR SINS!!! SEE THIS SPESHUL MAN HEEL THE SICK GIVE THE BLIND SITE AND RASE THE DED!!! And then the address, barely legible.

I tore off the poster, folded it tightly, and stuck it in my back pocket. At that moment, an elderly man with black skin and a gray Afro shouted, Hey boy, you can't do that! That there is public property. You can't steal no public property.

It's just a sign, I said. I'll return it.

See that you do so!

He approached me slowly, his left leg dragging behind his right. On his face he wore a pair of Pince-nez glasses. Strangely, his eyes were blue.

I don't suppose you know where this is, do you? Where I can find this Messiah?

Oh, him? He's a fraud, a phony. Doesn't do a goddamn thing. You'd have just as good luck praying to the Easter Bunny or Santa Claus. I wouldn't waste your money, boy.

I don't have any money to waste.

Oh, yes, I know that feeling well, believe me I do. Well, if you're so inclined, you can find him over at the Stockton Grounds. That's where they hold the carnival and where they keep the Messiah and the rest of the freaks...

I'd like to talk to him, I said. He might be the only one who can help me.

He ain't gonna help you, I promise you that. He's a fraud and a drunk. Them stories about him are hype and nothing more. He's got a promoter, you see. Hunter Timilli. You know his kind. A real snake oil salesman.

I realize it's probably a lost cause, I said. Everything. But I don't know who else to turn to.

I'll take you there, the man said. Sure, what else I got to do? The old woman is giving me hell every time I walk through the front doors. Only 'cause I got an appetite for the young girls.

I didn't want him to explain further and told him so. And so we walked, all around us brick and cement and busted windows and train tracks and stray cats and overfed crows.

This town, I said, is hard to figure.

Yeah, what you mean?

So much sin. So much guilt. So much hatred.

Factory Town

He nodded his head. Yes, mister, that's true. But it ain't different from any other place in the world. It ain't that the people are bad. It's just that we're scared. And fear makes people act in terrible ways.

And then my companion pointed up ahead, and sure enough there was a carnival, and just like everything else in this town, it was dead, dead, dead.

A metal fence surrounded the property, but it was collapsed, and soon I was inside the carnival grounds, and my companion walked in the other direction, shouting, It's hard to be saved for eternity, don't you know it?

And so I perused the grounds and I was wild-eyed and shivering. Here's what I saw: a giant Ferris wheel, most of the cars crooked and hanging on for dear life, the top of the ride disappearing into the mist; a carousel, the music long since quieted, paint peeling from the animals; bumper cars, sinking into the muck and mire; a giant clown face, grinning sinisterly, head bobbing in the wind; a house of mirrors, darkened forever. But nobody was on the carnival rides; everybody was watching the sideshow freaks.

It was true: I hadn't seen a crowd like this since my arrival in Factory Town. Men and women of all sorts, wearing factory uniforms and tuxedoes, ragged sweatshirts and evening dresses. They clamored around the cages where the sideshow freaks were housed. And the barker, with his top hat, shouting out: Ladies and gentlemen, step right up! The Stockton Carnival is proud to present: Freaks and Wonders! The most incredible people in the world! You'll see Three-Eyed Bill! You'll see the world's tallest female! She's over eight feet tall! You'll see the ugliest

Jon Bassoff

woman in the world! Fun for the whole family! Make sure to visit Wally the Walrus Man. He has whiskers on his face and flippers for his arms! And don't forget to check out the sad case of Harry Becker. He was born without a brain! Yes, ladies and gentlemen, you'll see 'em all here: Gwyneth the Four-Legged She-Man, Wyatt the Human Owl, Beatrice the Bearded Lady, Gil the Lion-Faced Lad, Shelly the Camel Woman, El Hoppo the Human Frog, Atasha the Lady Gorilla, Edmund the Texas Giant, Otto the Human Cigarette Factory, Sir Dickie the Penguin...

And so on and so on.

It was a ten-in-one and the acts were performed on a platform with the crowd moving from one to the other in order. The spectators were led through each of the ten acts by a midget named Marcus, and at the end of the acts each paying customer was given a miniature Bible and an ancient coin. Meanwhile, the barker was continually drumming up business with the help of the freaks themselves: see the Penguin Boy sit on his shoulders, flapping his little black wings.

But there was no interest in any of this for me, and I pushed my way through the crowds and freaks, during the course of which I was offered the chance to receive fellatio from a one-hundred-twelve-year-old woman or the chance to converse with a young man both blind and mute, but I declined each and every offer.

And then finally to the back corner of the carnival, where a fat man with a bowler's hat sat crosslegged on the ground, and behind him, in a narrow cage, wearing nothing but a tunic, his body covered

Factory Town

with tattoos made to look like a skeleton, lying in the corner, eyes empty and glazed, Miguel Romero, the Messiah.

CHAPTER 10

I was the only customer. All the noise and commotion regarding the other freaks? Not here. They left the Messiah alone. Nobody had much use for him. In fact, his promoter seemed surprised that somebody would show up at all. Ah, yes, yes, he said. Behold! Standing before your eyes is our Messiah, the human incarnation of God almighty! See what Miguel Romero can do for you! Do you suffer from an illness? He can help! Have you gone lame or blind? Have no fear—the mighty Miguel will heal you! Or perhaps you are depressed. Perhaps you have lost a loved one. This, ladies and gentlemen, is Miguel the Messiah's greatest trick. For the right price, he will bring your loved one back to the land of the living! Indeed, you will not find any prices better in Factory Town or anywhere else! Gone to a doctor and found a better offer? Or some street corner miracle worker?

Factory Town

Well, I say this to you. We will match any offers. You heard me right! Bring in a quote from your health care provider, or from your psychologist, or your psychic, and we will match or beat their price. Not only that. Miguel Romero is a true miracle worker, not some fly by night prophet. Indeed, was it not he who gave Dorothy Pendleton sight after she had been blind for nearly her entire life? Was it not he who brought back young Timothy Clifton after that horrendous car accident? Was it not he who has cured leprosy, syphilis, and polio? Won't you allow him to perform his latest miracle on *you*?

I approached slowly and the promoter pounced on me, placing his arm around my shoulder. And what about you, good sir? What can the Messiah do for you?

I'm looking for a girl. I was hoping he could help me find her.

A girl? Here in Factory Town?

Yes. My sources tell me—

But of course the Messiah can help you! Why wouldn't he be able to help you? A simple request. Much easier than curing syphilis! Twenty dollars, my good sir. That's my lowest price. Twenty dollars and he'll help you find your girl.

I reached into my pocket, pulled out my last crumpled twenty-dollar bill, and handed it to the promoter. He stuck it into his shirt pocket and nodded his head. I thank you, good sir, he said. You shall now have your moment with God.

A large key hung around his neck, and he used it to unlock the cage. I assumed he was going to summon Mr. Romero, but instead he indicated that I was to enter the cage alone. Feeling more than a little uneasy, I entered the cage and slowly started walking toward where the Messiah lay. I heard the door close and lock behind me. From somewhere a giant curtain fell, enveloping the entire cage and making it dark and difficult to see.

I stepped over banana peels and empty cans of beans. Sketchpads and prescription vials. Romero's eyes remained shut as I inched closer and closer. I'd never seen anybody like him. His entire body, face included, was covered with tattoos in the form of the human skeleton. On top of his head there was an opening in the skull tattoo revealing another tattoo of a brain. His insides for all to see. I squatted down and cleared my throat. He didn't open his eyes.

My name is Russell Carver. I was told you might be able to help me.

No movement.

There's a girl. Her name is Alana. I have a picture. I have reason to believe that she is here in Factory Town. I also have reason to believe that she is in serious trouble.

At this, Romero's eyes opened to slits, but he remained reclined, offering no signs of comprehension.

There are some strange happenings in this town, I continued. I'm beginning to think that Alana is not the only child in danger. I'm beginning to think that there are many, many children that are missing. And yet, everybody in this town seems to turn away at any such mention. The apathy and helplessness is startling. I feel so alone. But maybe you could…help me.

I waited a long time and Romero didn't say any-

Factory Town

thing. Outside I could hear carousal music and laughter and screams. The muffled voice of the barker. A human cannonball fired. Then, just when I was about to give up, Miguel Romero spoke. His voice was that of a child, barely intelligible.

I leaned forward. I'm sorry. What did you say?

He blinked a few times and shook his head sadly. I said that it doesn't matter. There isn't a thing I can do...

But there is, I said. There must be. Your promoter told me about the things you've done. Curing the blind, the lame...

No. I'm through with all that. I'm through helping people.

I stared into his eyes: empty, vacuous. I could feel the anger beginning to swell in my chest. This little girl, I said, is innocent. I know that there are a lot of terrible people in this town, in this world, but this girl is innocent. Are you just going to let her die?

He shrugged his shoulders. I guess I will, he said. There's nothing for me to do anymore. Just leave me be.

So that's it, huh? I said. That's all I'm going to get out of you?

Maybe if you come back another day...

They were right. You are a fraud. You are a phony.

He shook his head. Not a phony. I'm not pretending to be something I'm not. My promoter. He's the one. He's the phony.

Please, please! You need to help me! This girl, Alana, she's in great danger! And without her I can't go on. I just can't. And what about Charlie's mother? She's dying before our very eyes, withering into

Jon Bassoff

nothingness!

But Miguel Romero, the Messiah, wasn't listening to a thing I said. And soon he began to reminisce, talking about the good old days, tears rolling down his ink scarred cheeks. He said: Back in the good ol' world, things were different. They came from near and far to witness my magic. And magic I performed. A boy suffered from polio. Both of his legs were withered. I placed my hands on his legs. I prayed to the father in heaven. And instantly he was healed. The polio, gone forever. An elderly woman, blind since birth, her eyes rolled back into her head. Imagine, imagine! Never having seen a sunrise. Never having seen the wheat fields sway in the breeze. Never having seen a loved one's smile. Never having seen the stars or the moon or the sky. And I gave her vision. And it was my face that she saw first. But it was too much for her. She wanted me to make her blind again...

But these miracles were only done to make people believe. To show them that I was the one. And I asked them to leave behind their lives of sin. To live holy lives. To leave behind worldly possessions and follow me. Nobody listened. Not a single person. They left me alone to rot in this cage. Just another freak show. It's this town, you see. It's the Cowboy. It's hopeless, all hopeless.

And now my anger was building, ready to spill over. No! I shouted. This is no time to give up! This is no time to abandon the world!

But he only shook his head and stared at me with contempt. He said: Listen, mister, whoever you are. It might be easy for someone like you who hasn't

Factory Town

seen the full sickness of humanity to say, Don't give up. But when you have seen millions of human beings living like swine, living in depravity, the result of manifest poverty, while the royalty of our society sip Armand de Brignac champagne and smoke Hoyo de Monterrey cigars; when you have seen children living in maggot-infested apartment buildings while their mother is out whoring her body to the highest bidder; when you've seen a black man tied up to the back of a truck and dragged through town until his skin is peeled off his chest and face, his right arm ripped right from his body; when you've seen a woman raped by sixteen men, each of them taking turns bashing her face in and tearing apart her pussy; when you've seen a man poisoned with Tetrachlorodibenzodioxin, his face disfigured (jaundiced, pockmarked, and bloated); when you've seen a mayor molest hundred of pre-pubescent boys, threaten to kill them if they come forward; when you've seen a trusted confidant and friend rape your sister and castrate your brother; when you've seen a young girl, no more than eight years old, performing humiliating and degrading sexual acts on a balding investment banker; when you've seen pedophiliac clergymen debase and sodomize a thousand children; when you've seen a woman murder each of her five children by drowning them in the bathtub one by one, ignoring their pleas for mercy; when you've seen another mother dump her newborn baby in the landfill and then meet her friends for a night of dancing; when you've seen a pair of men stalking the Virginia-Maryland beltway for 47 days, randomly firing at motorists, killing 16 at least; when you've seen a young

Jon Bassoff

man and his girlfriend promising to give a homeless man lodging for the evening and then, once back at their suburban house, gouge out his eyes, stab him in the stomach, and poke into his exposed brain with a screwdriver, laughing and joking all the while; when you've seen a baby boy discovered beneath a bridge inside of a bassinet's box, his arms folded across the stomach, his fingernails trimmed neatly, his heart and liver and lungs removed — then you will understand, dear sir, why all is hopeless.

I didn't know what to say. I didn't know what to do. So I attacked him. Yes, I dove headfirst into the so-called Messiah and let loose with a torrent of blows to the body, to the face, a lifetime worth of anger and impotence and frustration manifesting itself into a single moment. At first he tried holding me off, but after a while, he stopped fighting, went limp, turned the other cheek. By the time I was done with him, his face was nothing more than a pulpy mess, and he lay on the ground, asking why had his father forsaken him.

I rose to my feet, wiped off his blood on my pants. I'll do it alone, I said, and walked toward the front of the cage.

Hunter Timilli, the promoter, was waiting for me, yanking off the curtain and unlocking the door. And how was it? he asked. Were you satisfied with my product?

I gave him a shove and he tripped over his feet, tumbling backwards. Now just wait one second, mister! he shouted, but I was already gone, walking back through the carnival, head blasted to pieces. As I walked, I could hear him cry out: Mon Dieu! What have you done to him? What have you done to my savior?

*   *   *

On the carnival grounds, pandemonium was ensuing. The freaks had escaped from their cages and were rebelling against their masters. It was a riot, the likes of which hadn't been seen for some time, if ever.

The dwarfs and the ogres, the deformed and the disabled, the insane and the imbecilic, were running or staggering or limping around the carnival, tearing down signs and crapping on the walls and banging their heads on the pavement and stabbing customers with sivs, and screaming and crying and shrieking.

Throats were cut and blood was spilled, and I pushed my way through the crowd, stepping over bodies, negotiating with sideshow freaks. How'd you like a kiss? said a woman with a two-foot beard.

What'll you do after I eat your liver, eat your brain? said a man with wings and a bird's beak.

Nyaaaaa! Nyaaaaa! said another man with clubbed feet and a missing eye and baby arms.

Great God has risen! I shouted and it was nighttime again, but the moon and the stars were missing as usual. Faces in the crowd were panicked; it was a terrible way to die, slaughtered by strangers and freaks, and people act like cowards when their lives are threatened, falling down on their knees and begging for mercy, using the meek as human shields, ratting out others.

Hours passed, and I made it through the riot, a little worse for wear, clothes torn and tattered, temple

Jon Bassoff

bleeding again, a concussion a near certainty.

And then something caught my eye. A woman, wearing a long flower dress, a dendrobium orchid in her ebony hair, a strand of costume pearls strangling her neck. She walked slowly past the abandoned Ferris wheel, as if in a dream. Somewhere a coyote was wounded, barking through the blood. And she kept walking, through the cold and mist, and the crows circled overhead. And it occurred to me that I knew who she was. Yes, it occurred to me that she was my long lost love.

CHAPTER 11

I followed her. She was alone and she was anxious. She walked hurriedly, pausing every so often to glance over her shoulder. And each time I would hold my breath, vanish into the shadows. Is somebody there? she said in a voice barely louder than a whisper. Nothing but stillness. She continued walking.

What terror! Never before had the sky been so dark; never before had the world been so lonely. A beer can tumbled down the street. Off in the distance, shrieks of laughter. The woman shivered, pulled her jacket tighter. A couple staggered down the middle of the street, both very drunk, he singing "Auld Lang Syne," nearly knocking my love down. The man turned back around, said, Sorry lady. You got something to drink? Some hashish perhaps? Then he laughed and laughed.

Jon Bassoff

She continued walking and my exhaustion and hunger were becoming real liabilities. I felt lightheaded and was having trouble focusing. She walked along broken sidewalks and through darkened alleyways and across a rickety old bridge. And on the bridge she stopped and stared down at the water crashing below, and then she hung her head and began to cry, and it was heartbreaking and beautiful, and I wanted so badly to comfort her, to pull her close and kiss away the tears, but I couldn't, not yet.

This was the way of the world, and eventually she continued walking, and I knew that her heart was ruptured beyond repair, arteries and ventricles gushing blood. Before too long we were back in the town center, standing outside the same filthy hotel that the whore had dragged me to. And how long ago that seemed!

Outside the hotel there were now a dozen or more tents, and a group of ragged-looking gypsies gathered around a makeshift bonfire, rubbing their hands in front of the fire. A large woman, 300 pounds at least, was nursing a man, her husband perhaps. A man wearing a stocking hat and nothing else was playing an oboe, haunting music. A sickly soothsayer was throwing down tarot cards, dooming everybody to damnation. The woman from my past dodged all of the people, all of the commotion, and made her way into the building. I waited a couple minutes and then tried to follow.

Before I could enter, however, I felt a sturdy hand on my shoulder, and then a baritone voice saying: Factory Town still treating you fairly, Mr. Carver?

I looked up and saw the square-jawed, Fu-Man-

Factory Town

chu wearing sheriff from the card game. He tipped his hat and gave me a big shit-eating grin. Good evening, Sheriff, I said. I can't talk right now. Something very important has come up.

Yes, yes. I'm sure it has. So tell me. Any luck in finding that girl? What was her name? Allison?

Alana. No, I haven't found her. But I think I've found somebody who might know where she is. That's why I need to go. She just went into the hotel...

Yes, mister, I've got my men hard at work, hitting the pavement, asking questions, searching for clues. Magnifying glasses out, pipes lit, you understand what I'm saying?

Yes, but really Sheriff—

You see, here in Factory Town, we take care of our own. A little girl missing— that won't do. I've got all my men on the case. Every one of my resources. You think somebody took her, do you?

I don't know. That's what I'm trying to find out. That's why I'd like to—

I tell you something, we've got our share of suspects here in Factory Town, don't you think? I mean, gawddaggit, every person here is capable of evil, real evil. Some of the things I've seen I wouldn't want anybody else to see.

And what have you done to stop it?

At this the sheriff laughed a big hearty laugh. I don't suppose I've done too much. Sometimes you gotta let the forest burn...

Suddenly, I felt an overwhelming revulsion for this man and for this town.

I need to go, I said and tried moving past the burly lawman.

I don't think that would be a good idea.

The hell are you talking about?

Christ, Carver, have you seen your temple? It looks pretty gruesome. That bandage is falling off, and I suspect you'll become delusional within hours...

No, just leave me alone. My head is fine. I need to talk to this woman.

I can't let you do that. You're too sick. I'm gonna take you to the doctor. That's the prudent thing to do, don't you think?

No, I—

But before I could say anything else, two deputies smelling of cheap bourbon and whore perfume came up behind me and grabbed my arms. I shouted out to the gypsies and the rest of the freaks outside the hotel for help, but they just sighed and shook their heads.

Take 'em to Dr. Byrd, the sheriff said. Get that wound taken care of.

So that's the way it was. They dragged me through the streets, stopping every so often to punch me in the solar plexus or elbow me in the jaw. And along the way, groups of people lined up like a parade, with their American flags and noisemakers and wind-chapped faces. They all smiled and waved, and the pretty ladies whispered behind their hands.

Eventually, we came to an old brown brick building, three stories, with rusted catwalks and crooked antennas and boarded-up windows. Much of the outside walls were covered with strange graffiti art including a Stalin-like portrait of a man in full cowboy gear, his face fully shadowed by his hat. The Cowboy.

I was taken inside to what must have once been a

Factory Town

hospital. Now the place was in disrepair, dead leaves and broken glass and dead birds covering the filthy linoleum floor. The walls were white-tiled, smeared with grime and blood. A wheelchair was in the middle of the hallway, lying on its side as if it had been shot dead by a sniper.

The waiting room is just down the hallway, one of the deputies said, his speech slurred from too many on-duty whiskies.

We walked through a heavy wooden door hanging off its hinges, and entered the waiting room. Here the linoleum floor had been pulled out completely, leaving only gray cement. There was a large metal desk and a metal chair, empty. Behind the desk, an oversized filing cabinet left ajar, patients' records spilling onto the floor. And other relics scattered: a child's doll, its eyeless head dangling from its body; a toy truck, the wood badly rotted; several magazines from decades earlier. And sitting on the floor, leaning against the cold concrete wall, a dozen or more women, sobbing, fondling rosaries, praying, mumbling, cutting skin. From outside the room, in the corridor, echoed the screams of the maimed.

The deputies told me to sit and I did so, in the corner away from the row of despairing women. I picked up one of the files that was lying on the floor and opened it up. On the top a date: July 11th, 1916. And the patient's name: Pete Beverly. Entered Jan'y 29/10. Diagnosis on day of admittance: Homicidal Mania. Has never attempted to kill anyone here. Is kept in a separate cell at night. Speaks of two men whom he is said to have killed in the parish prison. Considers his deed as the most natural, and finest ever performed by any one. Is unable to keep up a conversation for five minutes. Jumps from one subject to another. Is to all appearances quiet and inoffensive. Always night and day, has a nail, bent in a special manner, in his mouth. In killing these men, he undoubtedly did so through an irresistible instinctive impulse. He is of a jovial, kind, well-disposed, serviceable and amiable disposition...

I dropped the file on the ground, gazed up at the women. Many of them appeared to be pregnant, rubbing the protrusions in their bellies. *There are no children in this town.*

Meanwhile, one of the deputies struck up a conversation with one of the women, a very attractive brunette, no bump yet but still caressing her stomach. So ya got knocked up again, did you? he said, a snarl on his face.

She didn't answer, just nodded her head slowly.

Who fucked you this time?

Still no answer.

Who was it? Mike Pelfry? Gordan Thomas? Anthony Rider? Goddamn whore. And he slapped her on the face.

All of the other women remained against the wall, staring straight ahead, expressionless.

I tried rising to my feet, tried coming to her aid, but the other deputy shoved me against the wall, pulled out his .44 Special and pointed it at my forehead.

The hell are you doing? I said. You're a deputy! You're supposed to be protecting!

He grinned, revealing a mouthful of rotting teeth. Then, without warning, he slapped the barrel of the

Factory Town

gun hard against my nose. Immediately blood gushed out, spilling into my mouth and onto my clothes. I was dazed and confused, disheartened and unable.

Meanwhile, the first deputy, the drunkard with the red hair and the dead eyes, moved on to the next girl and the one after that, berating and slapping, taunting and kicking. There was nothing I could do. Except...

The deputy holding the pistol got distracted with the show his partner was putting on. He turned and watched, grinning the grin of a sociopath. I wasted no time. In a single movement, I rose to my feet and grabbed for his arm, twisting it back until the gun clattered to the floor. I kicked the gun away and started in on the deputy. Unarmed he wasn't so tough. Just as I had done with the Messiah, I pounded and pounded until I felt my fist between his skin and bone. He was pleading for me to stop and his partner was just chuckling: spilled blood was good for a laugh or two, anyway. Meanwhile the women remained quiet and still, taking it all in, the violence, the meanness.

And I might have gone on and on, I might have kept after him until he was nothing but a worthless corpse, but then a man appeared in the doorway, and it was the doctor from the party, and he clapped his hands two times, and for some reason I stopped, hid my bloody hands beneath my shirt. Such a commotion, he said in a thin voice. Ah, well, such is the way of the world. Mr. Carver, I presume? I'll see you presently. Yes, yes, such is the way of the world.

CHAPTER 12

Dr. Byrd walked with a limp and breathed heavily as we made our way down the long corridor toward his office. He wore heavy platform shoes that echoed loudly in the hallway. There were no patients here, no nurses, no secretaries. I must apologize, he said, for the subpar conditions of my office building. Sanitation is certainly a concern. You see, I am terribly overworked and have little to no assistance. I had a custodian, nice fellow, Mexican, but he ended his life in the last puputan.

Puputan?

A Balinese term that means…

But it was at that very moment that a woman staggered out of a room, wearing a nightgown bespeckled with blood. Her black hair was long and wild, and her face was that of the dead.

Factory Town

Oh, my Lord! the doctor said, his voice suddenly frantic. Mary Lou, what in heavens are you doing out of your room? And what do you have in your arms all mangled and bloody? Oh Lord, oh Lord, help us all.

Put it back! she said, face changing into something terrible. Please, doctor! Put it back!

Darling, darling, it's too late for that. You really shouldn't have gone poking around into those bins. Terrible! I wish it didn't have to be this way, you must believe me. It's the Cowboy and his *Book of Edicts*. A travesty, I say, an absolute travesty! But what can we do? You shouldn't have gone poking around, my dear girl. What's done is done. The town must die with us, so it is written!

And she began walking toward me slowly and I couldn't move; it was the most terrible thing I'd ever seen, bloody and dead, and she begged me to help her, please, please help her, but there was nothing I could do, the town must die with us...

In Dr. Byrd's office, more destruction. Graffitied walls crumbling down. Rubble everywhere. A hospital bed frame, no mattress. Operating lights dangling from the ceiling. On a wooden table, some sort of an antique operation kit, instruments badly rusted.

If you wouldn't mind lying down, he said, but there was no place to lie except the metal frame and I did so, sharp spikes digging into my skin. He turned on the hospital lights and I was blinded. Terrible wound, he said. Badly infected. How did this happen?

I don't know. Nothing makes sense.

In any case, we must get this taken care of. Unfortunately, flesh wounds are not my...specialty.

But you're a doctor.

True. But I was forced into this position. I am an insurance salesman by trade. When the Cowboy issued his edicts, he trained several of us in a particular bloody art. The other doctors are gone. Now it's just me. Overworked. And not qualified to make a judgment on your wound. But I would say infected. Certainly. I could write you a prescription. But for what? I haven't the slightest idea since I don't have pharmaceutical training. Perhaps if we just clean it with some lye...

I was taken by surprise. He pressed a cloth against the wound, and my skin was on fire, and I screamed. I tried pushing him away, but I was weakened by the pain, and he kept the chemical firmly pressed against my temple.

This is what we do to naughty boys, he said. It would be best, Mr. Carver, if you mind your own business from now on. Stop the poking around. You are not a dime store detective. You understand, *ja*? and now his accent was that of a German.

I nodded my head vigorously, sweat pouring down my face.

Dies ist gut, Mr. Carver, and he removed the cloth. I could feel the wound bubbling, my face forever disfigured. The doctor smiled at me. His teeth were sharp and narrow, his gums purple. Speaking again: But I just need to make sure...

He limped back to the middle of the room and removed a tool from his kit. On one end of the tool was some sort an old rusted drill bit. On the other end was a plastic handle. The doctor smiled. Braun's

Factory Town

Cranial Perforator, he said. You have heard of this device?

My hands were suddenly tied to the bedframe. Black magic. Dr. Byrd, the doctor, the masochist, placed the metal bit against my wound. And then he started twisting...

* * *

When I awoke, I was all alone. My hands were free, my head was bandaged. Dr. Byrd was nowhere to be found. His torture tools were gone. I sat up. My temple was pounding, shrapnel ricocheting in my skull.

I got to my feet and hobbled over to Dr. Byrd's desk. I opened the drawer and fumbled around for a while. A portfolio of photographs: fetuses recently extracted. Bloody faces, crushed skulls, missing limbs. And uncashed checks. Ten thousand here, sixteen thousand there. A letter from the Cowboy praising him for his dedication to the cause. A form letter to be sure.

* * *

Back in the hallway, now completely darkened. I couldn't even see my hand six inches in front of my face. I walked slowly, cautiously, hands reaching ahead into the blackness. I heard sounds. Rats screeching. A train horn, off in the distance. My own footsteps and breath...

I don't know how much time passed. I continued through the corridor, a blind man, feeling the walls for an exit, finding nothing but peeling paint and dampened concrete.

I began to panic, afraid that I would wander through the darkness forever. I tried shouting for help, but my voice left me and I couldn't make a sound. I was a man condemned, again and again.

And then I remembered Ms. Marcell from my childhood and the stories about her, told from generation to generation, how she stole children from their houses, tiptoed into their bedrooms and placed them in a gunny sack and then took them into the forest and buried them, still alive, and if you listened closely you could hear the muted screams through the dirt, and I never saw her except for once on a cold winter's evening when I'd wandered too far from my house, and she was standing at the end of the block beneath the glow of a streetlamp, and her hair was white and wild and her skin was pale, almost translucent, and she grinned and it was such a terrible grin, all the evil in the world in that grin, and she started walking toward me, her back all hunched, but still with that terrible grin, and I knew it would be the end of me, that I'd be in that burlap bag and I'd be beneath the dirt and I'd die and rot there, and I knew that I should run but I didn't move—a part of me wanted her to take me, to be damned forever— and she continued walking and I remained still, and then she stopped and glared at me and the grin faded away slowly, and there was nothing but blackness where her eyes should have been, but she came no closer, instead walking up her walkway, overgrown with weeds, and into her crumbling little house surrounded by shovels and sickles and chaff cutters and

Factory Town

breast plows, and her windows remained darkened until her death.

And now she was speaking in a hushed voice, I knew it was her: *I've had my eye on him... He's done some terrible things... We'll take him to the forest... Bring the pointed shovel... It won't be long now... We'll mark the grave with his teeth...*

I was on the precipice of sanity, certainly, and so it was a great relief when I saw the dull glow of a light up ahead. At first I thought it was some sort of a lantern hanging from the wall, but then I realized that the light was moving, swinging side to side, and no matter how far I walked I couldn't reach it.

I began jogging through the darkened corridor, wondering about the light, wondering about the sack woman, wondering about Alana, Alana, Alana, the last vestige of innocence.

And then soon I was out of breath, my lungs burning and my legs heavy. And still I kept running, on one occasion tripping over a jutted drain, smashing to the concrete floor.

Finally, I reached the light source. It was a very old man with a mining lantern hanging around his neck. He wore a black suit, badly torn, and was pushing some sort of a shopping cart with a tarp thrown over it. I shouted out to him, but he didn't turn around, just kept pushing the cart, one of the wheels spinning erratically. I lunged forward and grabbed his shoulder and he stopped, spun around. He was tall and undernourished, just like so many in this town, the features of his skull pushing against his skin. His gray eyes were bloodshot and sunken. He didn't say a thing.

Jon Bassoff

I was hoping, I said, that you could help me get out of this building. I've been wandering for a long time. Everything is dark. Everything is lonely. I'm tired and I'm hungry. I'm confused. I'm looking for a girl. Her name is Alana. I believe that she is in terrible danger. I believe I may have had my first real break in the case. I saw a woman who I recognized from long ago. She might know something. I'd like to talk to her. But I'm stuck here. I can't get out. I haven't slept for such a long time...

The man only grunted and then continued walking. I followed after him.

The world was falling apart, piece by piece. We walked for a long time, he leading, me closely behind. At some point he turned and handed me what appeared to be a dried fig, an odd gesture. I stuck it in my mouth, but it tasted rotten and so I spit it out. He smiled a toothless grin at that.

We came to a thick metal door. The old man pulled it open revealing a narrow and seemingly endless metallic staircase, ascending steeply. He grabbed the front of the shopping cart with one hand and pointed to the handle. I quickly realized that he wanted me to help him carry the cart. I nodded my head and got a good grip on the handle. The cart wasn't light and I was amazed that the old man was able to lift the front section.

Up, up, up we walked, our feet and the wheels of the cart echoing loudly on the metal stairs. Every so often we'd reach a platform with open steel gratings and we'd rest, but then he'd nod and grunt and we would begin our ascent again.

After this went on for some time, I began to get

Factory Town

frustrated and agitated. Once again, I'd been sidetracked from my mission. It seemed the harder I tried, the further away from answers I got.

And then, just when I was beginning to lose all hope, just when my anger was reaching a tipping point, we reached another door. The old man shoved it open and pulled the shopping cart behind him. With that familiar sense of dread, I followed. After a few steps, I realized that we were on the roof of the building, the crumbling little town below. The sky was dark. There were no stars, no moon. Standing in the middle of the roof was a group of people, all dressed in various hues of black. A woman with gray hair stretching to the ground sat on a stool and played a mournful song on a strange harp.

When the people saw the old man, they quickly rushed up to him and started hugging and comforting him.

It's so terrible, one of them said. Dead, dead!

Yes, yes, said another. Dead. He was a good man, a noble man.

And another: We must remember him in a positive light. We shouldn't let his occasional failings overwhelm his true nature.

A good man! Yes, he had failings. Don't we all?

They never proved a thing! Not beyond a reasonable doubt.

Confused, I approached a woman who wore a long black shawl and dark sunglasses. Excuse me, I said. But what is going on here?

She removed her sunglasses. One of her eyes was covered with an eye patch. The other was badly swollen. Isn't it terrible? she said. He killed himself.

Jon Bassoff

Who killed himself?

She pointed to the shopping cart. The tarp had been removed. For a long while I just stood there, looking down at the profound sight. A naked body, the skin purple and waxy, blood pooling in his calves and feet, eyes sinking into his skull. A face unrecognizable, having been obliterated by a shotgun shell.

CHAPTER 13

The old man, a deaf mute, moaned mournfully, rocking back and forth. A pair of burly men walked across the tarred roof carrying a simple pine casket ornamented with a cross. They opened the lid and then carefully lifted the mangled corpse into the casket. They closed it shut. The woman playing the harp began singing in a haunted voice. It was a song I remembered from my childhood.

> *Oh, the Deacon went down to the cellar to pray*
> *He found a jug and he stayed all day*
> *Oh, the Deacon went down to the cellar to pray,*
> *He found a jug and he stayed all day*
> *Ain't gonna grieve my Lord no more.*

And then, after the song, one of the mourners, a very short man with blonde hair plastered onto his

Jon Bassoff

forehead, a pair of broken spectacles on the tip of his nose, and a walking cane in his gnarled right hand, stood on top of a ledge, cleared his throat, and began speaking in a quiet, reedy voice. The mourners immediately hushed and gave him full attention.

Here lies the body of a man, he said, banging his cane against the metal platform. He was a son and a husband. He laughed often and cried perhaps not enough. But now what do we do with him, now that he is trapped in this simple wooden casket, breath forever gone, skin and blood and muscle eventually decomposing, leaving only bones in that casket; a skull with a fleshless grin? I have been asked to pay tribute to him, to tell his story in some way. And, most importantly, to explain the circumstances surrounding that tragic day, nearly six years ago...

What you must know is that he came from a difficult childhood. A depressive mother. An abusive father. Yes, yes, who can forget the havoc his father wreaked on the town? Remember Tyler Yancey? How he tore off his ear and stomped on his face? Or Daniel McClure? Snapped his neck, left him a cripple. But the havoc he wreaked on the town pales in comparison to that of his own family. Physical and emotional. Year after year after year. And remember our own role, our own complicity. We sat in the tavern and drank our beers and tapped our fingers and spoke in hushed voices and listened to the screaming and the moaning and the pleading, and we didn't move from our chairs; we just sighed and hung our heads, and certainly that makes us guilty, too, condemned as well.

For we can only imagine what it was like for

Factory Town

him spending his whole life trying to avoid his father's horrific prognostication. Fearing that he was, indeed, a prophet of the devil. Do you understand this agony? Every time a seed of anger was planted in his gut he became petrified that this seed would grow into something unmanageable and unimaginable. He worried that he would lose control of his rationality and that the animalistic him would attack and assault while the old man sat at the kitchen table sipping whiskey and sharpening his work knife and laughing, laughing.

He was just a boy, don't you understand? Just a boy. His mother was six months pregnant. And she used to let him touch her stomach, feel the baby kicking. But the old man, he was bitter. And he got it into his head that he wasn't the father. He got it into his head that his wife was a whore and that the father was the plumber or the sheriff or the doctor or the minister or, God forbid, his own brother. And the irony, the terrible irony, is that the old man was fucking everything with a hole, including a girl who worked at the filling station who wasn't more than fifteen years old. But his wife was the whore, that's what he said.

And so this one night he came home, and he'd been drinking, and he was looking for a fight. And the boy was in his room reading his superhero comics, wishing that he had a power or two to stop him from hurting his mom. And as his father shouted, as his father berated his mother, the boy remained huddled in his bed, and he reached under the bed and pulled out his black mask and his plastic sword, and he tried getting the courage because he knew something bad was going to happen—he had premonitions, too.

Then he heard the sounds of furniture being overturned and walls being punched. And not long after, his mother screeching, sounding more like an animal than a human. He covered his ears with his hands, but he could still hear her. And his father, shouting, Who'd you fuck? Who'd you fuck, you little whore? You think I want another little bastard running around this filthy world? Fuck you! Fuck you, you goddamn whore!

The boy rose from his bed. Outside the rain was falling, crashing down on the tin roof. Thunder boomed and lightning flashed, lighting up his darkened boy's room. He wore a mask and a cape, he carried a sword, and still he trembled. But he knew that courage was challenging fear, not overcoming it. He opened the door and stood in the hallway, shrouded in the shadows. Slowly he walked. The thunder was so loud, the lightning so bright, that he feared the house would be destroyed. His hands wouldn't stop trembling. His teeth clattered metronome-style.

He walked down the hallway and through the living room. He came to their bedroom door, a sickly light glowing beneath. Cautiously, he turned the knob and pushed open the door. His eyesight became blurry. His head became dizzy. His mother was sitting on the floor, fully nude, rocking back and forth. His father stood in the middle of the room, gripping a large metal wrench. His white T-shirt was soaked through with blood. His cowboy hat lay on the chair. The man looked at the boy and his expression was that of the damned. It ends with us, he said. Don't

Factory Town

you get it, boy? It ends with us.

The boy raced out of the bedroom and out the front door and the rain pounded the pavement and he ran until he thought his chest would explode and then he found a ditch and he stumbled down there, shielded by black poplar trees, and he stayed there for a long time...

Years passed, and his mother died a terrible death (just skin and bones was she), and his father died by his own hand (nobody found him for nearly a week, and by the time a neighbor named Mrs. Wickland did discover him, the stink was so bad they had to have his old shack fumigated), but I fear those corpses were but illusions. Violence and sin and hatred passed from generation to generation. And so they were passed to him.

The son grew to be a man, and Lord knows he tried to avoid the cycle of violence. He left the filthy town of his childhood and moved to a quiet town of homogeneity. He got an honest job, a desk job. He met a woman and they fell in love, or at least they convinced each other that they were in love, and eventually they got married. He tried his best to be a good husband. This is undeniable. Happy days and loving nights. But he soon suspected a terrible truth: that his wife was a devilish woman with aims of destruction. Spitting on their vows. Whoring her body. Laughing in his face. Yes, he began to hear her having hushed conversations on the phone. He found suspicious receipts. He smelled unfamiliar colognes on her body. And he noticed her skittishness, the vestiges of guilt. How was he to handle this situation? How had his father handled the situation?

Jon Bassoff

When she told him that she was pregnant, the suspicions only intensified. He wasn't the father, he was sure of it. But without proof, without certainty, he hesitated to accuse…

And now I ask you to close your eyes and imagine. Picture the setting. A cold dark night. No moon. No stars. She was gone again. Missing from his bed. So he went searching. And when he finally found her, he saw that she was with that man from October Hill, the man with the bowler's hat and the vulture eye. They were drinking cherry brandy from mason jars and they were laughing, laughing.

He felt a terrible rage, and he knew this rage would be inside of him forever. He knew what he would do, what he had to do. He hid in the deep dark forest while the rain fell and the crows hovered. Hours passed and then she appeared and she was drunk, staggering down the path. When he stepped out from behind the boughs, she didn't recognize him because his face was hidden in the shadows. She gasped and placed her hand over her heart, but then she recognized him and a smile spread across her face and she said, Darling you scared me. You scared me terribly. He didn't say a thing, just took a step toward her and then another one. A man can only take so much. And so it was that he placed his hand around her neck and squeezed, and she was too weak and drunk to fight him, her face turning red and then purple, her eyes bulging. And when she was nearly dead, he released his grip and she fell to the ground, gasping for breath. He picked her up and slung her over his shoulder and walked toward that ancient well, hidden deep in the forest. Oh, how she

Factory Town

begged for her life, too late, too late, and he pulled her over the edge of the stones and down she fell into that darkened tunnel, down she fell.

Days passed and they came after him with torches and gunnysacks and rifles. And so he hid in a cheap motel that smelled of gasoline and cigarettes, and he paced back and forth like a caged animal, drinking bourbon, spitting up blood. A man can only take so much. And so a bullet to the head.

And with that the short man with the cane and the broken glasses stepped off the platform and disappeared into the crowd. The woman on the harp started playing and singing again:

From the land of yearning
To that without yearning
From the land of pity
To that without pity!

And then the same burly men that had carried and loaded the casket now lifted it and started walking across the roof as the rest of the crowd followed them in line. But there was no place to go; they reached the edge of the roof. Then they did something that caught me by surprise. Without warning, they started swinging the casket back and forth, back and forth. Then they heaved it off the roof. For what seemed to be an eternity, the casket floated in the black night before finally smashing against the pavement below, the wood cracking and splintering open, displaying the corpse in all his ghoulishness.

Not fifteen seconds after it smashed against the ground, several grotesque-looking men scurried onto the pavement and surrounded the casket. Many of the men were naked, and all were badly emaciated. I recognized one of them: Estaban from the party, from the card-playing room. The fellow with the chunk of meat that they'd forced me to eat. Ostrich meat, they'd called it. But there were no ostriches in Factory Town.

The crowd watched from the roof as the men, the Vultures, shrieked like banshees and, in a frenzy, pulled apart the casket. They used knives and scissors, scythes and sickles to tear at the body. Watching in horror, the mute gnashed his teeth and pulled his hair. Many other mourners sobbed and screamed, but all watched helplessly. Within thirty seconds, the body was torn apart completely, and the Vultures vanished into alleys and doorways and vestibules.

And then stunned silence. I turned to one of the mourners, a woman with a beak-like nose and beady blue eyes. Why? I said. Why did you throw the casket off the rooftop?

The woman looked at me like I was crazy. Why? Because we've always done it that way, that's why.

Well, what could I say to that? This town had rituals and traditions that made no sense, no sense at all. I was beginning to think there wasn't a single righteous person in this whole town...

And then another commotion among the mourners. A young woman, golden hair flowing in the night breeze, was standing on the edge of the roof, the next suicide. Take care of my mama! she shouted, tears rolling down her cheeks. And tell her I'm going to meet my Lord!

And with that she jumped, and her scream sound-

Factory Town

ed distant, otherworldly, and then she was sprawled on the ground, body contorted and bloody. I couldn't watch so I turned away, despair like a giant tarp thrown over me.

Madness overtook the mourners and things got out of control quickly. Other members of the group followed the young woman's lead and began jumping off the rooftop. A puputan, the abortionist had called it. Mass suicide. Every time I tried preventing one of them from leaping, talking them down, physically restraining them, another one would sneak past me and join the mangled and maimed on the asphalt landing below.

Not all jumped. Some slit their own throats with knives. Others came armed with guns. And still others took to pounding their heads against the cement wall. Death to them all.

Throughout, the harpist played, the music of the damned, and when she saw that they were all gone, she carefully placed her harp on its side, reached into her blouse and pulled out a very small bottle. She uncapped it, made the sign of the cross, and then swallowed it down. Her eyes remained closed for a minute, and her face was calm and peaceful. Then the poison took effect and she fell to her knees and then to her back and began convulsing uncontrollably, and it was a terrible thing to watch, a body being consumed by death, and soon blood appeared through the pores on her face, and her eyes bulged like in some kid's cartoon, and then she was still, other than her right foot which kept twitching for several minutes. Then it too was still.

Shrieks echoed through the streets and the Vultures returned, this time with wheelbarrows and barbed nets and burlap sacks, gathering the bodies, twenty at least, a forever feast, leaving behind only blood and torn clothing. I knew it would only be a matter of time before they arrived on the rooftop to finish their scavenging.

Overcome with a terrible sadness, I sat down, pulling my knees to my chest. The wind blew cold and the snow started falling again, specking my sleeve with white. I couldn't go on any further. I closed my eyes and felt a great wave of exhaustion spread through my body. Just to sleep, if only for a few minutes...

I could hear the Vultures coming up the metal stairs, footsteps and rabid yelps. And then I saw a woman walking slowly across the roof and she was the woman from the carnival, the woman I'd followed, the woman I once loved, and she too tried to leap but I wouldn't let her. I pulled her close to me, and I could feel her trembling, and she flailed against me, trying to escape my arms, trying to escape this world, and her eyes were sad, so sad, and her lips were soft, and I kissed her, and without beauty, we are lost, and we have nothing to do but sin and hate, hate, hate.

CHAPTER 14

Time stayed still and then the Vultures arrived and they were human, but hardly so, storing up the scattered bodies for the winter. I grabbed the woman's hand and we raced across the roof, snow falling harder. The Vultures weren't interested in us; in fact, they fell to the ground and huddled against one another in fear as we rushed past them.

We made our way into the staircase and started down, our feet echoing loudly on the metallic stairs. And once again everything was dark and once again I was lost and once again hope was fading fast. But the woman sensed my incertitude and pulled me forward. I know the way, she said.

We came to one of the staircase platforms and she stopped and placed her finger on her lips, even though I hadn't been speaking. She got down on her knees and it was then that I saw a narrow opening in the wall. This is the quickest way, she said. At first I didn't think that it would be wide enough for either of us to crawl through, but the woman got down to her stomach and pulled herself through, vanishing momentarily from sight. I thought about the rats and cockroaches that must be making this strange tunnel their home, and I hesitated to enter. But then I heard terrible screams echoing in the stairwell, and I fell to my stomach and entered after her.

The tunnel was dark and I couldn't see the woman, my companion, but I heard her voice, encouraging me to follow. At first the tunnel was extremely narrow and I felt claustrophobic, fearful that I would become stuck, but after a while the tunnel widened enough for me to get on my haunches and then to stand upright, only slightly hunched. My eyes adjusted to the darkness, and it soon became obvious that we were no longer in the building. The walls and floor of the tunnel were made of rock and dirt nearly completely iced over. We were underground, travelling like moles.

There were no footprints in the dirt, and I found that disturbing. Cold breath spewed from my mouth and I couldn't stop shivering. Where are we? I shouted out. Where are we going? But the woman didn't hear me or, if she did, didn't bother answering.

And so I followed. Water dripped from the ceiling and bats flew past, shrieking in rage. On the ground I saw artifacts of mining days past: An ore bucket connected to a long metal chain. A miner's hat and pick. A rotted wheelbarrow. And still the woman walked, her dress and hair swaying like in some long forgotten dream.

Factory Town

By the time we finally reached the end of the tunnel, my legs were sore, and I felt dizzy and exhausted. My companion stepped out of the tunnel and for the first time since I'd entered Factory Town, the sun was shining. She smiled and said, Here we are! We made it, darling!

I stepped outside and looked around, my eyes adjusting to the sudden brightness. We were now in a suburban neighborhood lined with endless rows of identical houses, young trees mostly bare, leaves scattered across the empty asphalt. A neighborhood I knew well.

The woman pointed to one of the houses. 3155 Winding Brook Circle. An American flag hung proudly from the front of the house. A sign hung on the door: HOME IS WHERE THE HEART IS. There were four planters filled with flowers, a rocking chair, wind chimes. The woman wiped a wisp of hair from her face, smiled broadly. Wait until you see what I've done with the house, she said. Just you wait and see! I got a new tablecloth for the dining room and a lovely new coffee table for the living room. The table was on sale for eighty-nine dollars. Can you believe it? Eighty-nine dollars! This is our home, Russell, and you're just going to love it!

* * *

So I moved to the suburbs.

Life was slow and calm and comfortable. I pruned the bushes and got a job in sales. I waxed the floors and shopped at Wal-Mart. I mowed the lawn and brought the trashcans out on Tuesday mornings.

Jon Bassoff

The woman took good care of me. She made wonderful dinners (steak and potatoes, pasta and salad, burger and fries) and did several loads of laundry a day. She watched her figure and got naked occasionally. She enjoyed romantic comedies and read cooking magazines and took Xanax. We were so happy together.

I asked her if she wanted to have a date night. Just like old times. Grab a bite to eat at Red Lobster and then catch a movie. *Heaven Can Wait*, maybe. Or the new *Superman*, staring Christopher Reeve and Gene Hackman.

Oh, darling, I'd love to, but I'm working on knitting that sweater for you. I'd like to have it done by your birthday. Why don't you go? Maybe call some of your friends? Grab a drink afterwards? That'll also give me some time to vacuum the carpets and clean the bathrooms. They haven't been cleaned in three days. And with a man in the house…

I thought things over. Okay, I said. If you don't mind. I guess I'll go after dinner. Maybe invite ol' Charlie. I haven't seen him in ages.

That's a wonderful idea, she said. After dinner, then. Speaking of which, do you have any preferences? I was thinking of making a lasagna, but I could switch to beef brisket if you're in the mood.

I shook my head and grinned. I love your lasagna, darling. Of course, you could make a pile of shit taste good.

And she wore a white apron and a blue dress and high heels. And her face and hair were perfectly made up. And she loved her self-cleaning oven and her automatic dishwasher and her rotating vacuum

Factory Town

cleaner and her electric mixer.

While she cooked, I watched football and drank Miller from cans. The Broncos beat the Chargers. Craig Morton threw for two touchdowns, one to Jack Dolbin and one to Riley Odom. The Orange Crush did their part—Gradishar was all over the place.

Soon the woman called me to dinner. Everything was perfect. There was a bouquet of flowers on the table and a bottle of champagne on ice. She took a thin slice of lasagna for herself but gave me a real man's portion. And when I was done, we talked about agreeable things: the weather, the decorations, her hair.

Everything was pleasant, and I watched the snow fall gently to the ground. Factory Town seemed so far away, so distant. Factory Town. Just the thought of it caused my anxiety to return. I pushed my plate out of the way and rose to my feet, a bit unsteadily.

Darling? she said. What's the matter? You look a little panicked.

And then suddenly, the photograph was in my hand and I was waving it around. This girl, I said. Her name is Alana. She's gone missing. I've been entrusted with finding her.

The woman looked up and smiled, her eyes blinking rapidly. She took a sip from her coffee and said: That's nice, dear.

From what I can gather, she's here in Factory Town, and she's in terrible danger. If I don't find her soon, I fear she'll die. This is no time for rest. Time is running out.

Mm-hmm. Darling, you're almost done with your beer. Would you like another one? Would you like some more soufflé?

Listen to me, I said. I need your help. Don't you understand? I can't do this alone.

Help?

Finding this girl. Do you have any information? Do you know where she is?

The smile remained frozen on her face. After several moments, she shook her head and said: No. Of course not. I've never heard of Alana.

I placed the photograph on the table in front of her. She didn't look down, instead staring straight ahead with that empty grin. Look at this picture, I said. It's a computer-generated image. It shows the way she might look today. They're very good at this type of thing, nowadays.

She looked down at the photograph and studied it for short while. Then she looked up. Darling, it's getting late. Aren't you supposed to meet Charlie?

What?

For the movie. Aren't you meeting him at the movies?

Yes. But right now... that is to say...

I'll take care of the dishes. You have fun tonight. Don't worry about what time you get home. Take your time. I'll just be knitting...

I didn't know what to say. She'd gotten me all flustered. The woman knew something, that much was sure. She was just like everybody else in this town with her share of secrets, terrible secrets...

Oh Lord, she said, I almost forgot to tell you. They're having a huge sale at Wal-Mart this weekend. Perhaps we could get you a new tie. The old one is fraying at the seams. And I sure could use a new

Factory Town

apron.

Well, this sudden swarm of trivialities was making me good and irate. Quickly, suddenly, I grabbed a hold of the woman's wrist and gripped it tightly. I leaned in closely so I could see the pores on her face. When I spoke, my teeth remained clenched and my hands trembled. I don't think you understand the gravity of this situation! I shouted. I'm not fucking around here! If we don't do something, this girl will die!

The woman tried rising to her feet, but I squeezed her wrist tighter and she gasped in pain. Darling, she said. You need to let go of my wrist. You don't...you don't want to end up like your father, do you? You don't want his prophecy to come true, do you?

So that's what this was about. I glared at her, my grip remaining firm, and I noticed that she had the same empty eyes as the whore, that she was no different, no different at all.

You've got some nerve, I said, my voice barely louder than a whisper.

Let go of my wrist.

I nodded my head slowly and then released my grip. She smiled stiffly and massaged her wrist, bent it back and forth.

Now, she said, I need to get started on the dishes. Do you need anything else? A glass of port? A cigar?

No, I said. I'm fine.

The woman, nothing but a stranger, straightened out her dress and began stacking the dishes, her bouffant perfectly quaffed. I watched her, never took my eyes off her. And then that old sense of dread rose through my body, and suddenly I remembered, remembered the terrible things I'd done, and I'd pay, we all pay.

*   *   *

Charlie Gardner, my childhood friend, was waiting in the lobby of the theatre with a large Pepsi in one hand and a larger popcorn in the other, cradled against his chest. He grinned when he saw me, said, I'm surprised you managed to get out of the house, you domesticated son-of-a-bitch!
What are you talking about?
What do you think I'm talking about? Mrs. Piper Carver has turned you into a regular lapdog.
Mrs. Carver…
We walked through the lobby, and things were peculiar. There were no moviegoers. No ushers. The neon refreshment lights were flashing aggressively, but there was nobody behind the counter. I wondered where Charlie had gotten his popcorn and soda. Nobody was there. Nobody at all.
We didn't have tickets but it didn't matter. There was nobody to collect them. We walked down the darkened hallway, past several auditoriums where movie screens flickered and soundtracks blasted, but all empty of people.
Charlie didn't seem bothered by the odd scene, or perhaps he hadn't noticed. He talked about work and sports and women. That's the thing you've got to realize, buddy. They're all sluts. Every damn one of them. It's such a shame, too…
And then we finally came to the auditorium where Superman flashed on the marquee. I followed

Factory Town

behind Charlie as he wandered into the middle of the last row of the empty movie theatre. He sat down and placed his feet on the chair in front of him, and I sat down next to him. He kept on talking. I couldn't stand him, never had, never had. Goddamn whores is all they are. You don't believe me? You should see some of the shit these girls will do. And I'm talking about the nice ones. In the mouth. Up the ass. It don't matter. Piper even. You think she's so innocent? Nah. She's just like all the others. Born to fuck. Born to betray. You think she's at home knitting you a goddamn sweater? You're a goddamn fool! You've always been a goddamn fool!

I didn't know what Charlie was talking about, and I didn't know how to respond. I guess I should have shouted at him or pushed him or hit him. But I didn't do anything. I just sat there while he continued berating me, berating Mrs. Carver.

Don't you get it, Russell? She's never been true to you. Not for a single day. She's played you for a fool. You working your butt off, trying to make a better life for the both of you. While she goes from bed to bed, ass in the air, getting fucked by everybody in the goddamn neighborhood.

That's not fair. She...

You think Frank Delaney was the only one? Is that what you think? Shit, Russell. You're stupider than I thought. Hell, even I fucked her! Does that surprise you, buddy? Well, you've gotta figure things out, but quick. And now you've got a little taste of what your old man had to deal with. Now you can understand a bit, can't you? You know what's gonna happen, don't you? One of these days, you're bound to turn into the

Jon Bassoff

old bastard! *You even look like him. You have the same eyes.*

And then the lights dimmed and the previews started. Charlie grinned like nothing had happened, and then he ate his popcorn and drank his soda, and this was the strangest theatre I'd ever been in...

* * *

The movie was tragic, so tragic. Lois Lane suffocating beneath dirt and debris. Superman, unwilling to use his power to travel back in time, heeding his father's warning to never interfere with human history. The movie ending with Superman weeping over her crushed body. Meanwhile, I couldn't help myself, and I began crying too. I cried and cried and I couldn't stop, and when I looked up Charlie was gone, and I had so many regrets; I was buried alive in them.

* * *

I made my way home, the suburban streets more hushed than usual. Porch lights glowing dully. Curtains closed. Blue lights flashing from television sets. There were no humans, no cars, no wind. I blew into my hands, trying to warm them. And then I sat outside the house, my house, behind a bush, watching and waiting, watching and waiting, and I drank more than I should have. The sky was dark and the stars were dead and gone, waiting for a burial.

Time passed, and a car came creeping down the street. It was out of place in the suburbs—a long

Factory Town

hearse, no longer black, now candy apple green. I was hoping the strange car would keep on moving, but I knew that it wouldn't. Sure enough, the driver pulled into the driveway and turned off the engine.

I ducked down further behind the bush, making sure that I was out of sight. I heard voices, drunken voices, but I was too anxious to peek for fear of being discovered. A few moments passed, and then I could hear the front door open and the lilting voice of Mrs. Carver. There was more laughter, and then the door slammed shut and all was quiet, that nightmarish suburban silence.

CHAPTER 15

I sat outside that house for a long time. I had a flask filled with cheap brandy, and so I drank and drank and drank, and then I thought about what might happen next and I shivered.

Voices again, whispering in my ear, and I rose from behind the bush and walked slowly down the path toward the house. I stood on the porch and the sign said HOME IS WHERE THE HEART IS. I turned the handle but it was locked. I pulled out a key from my shirt pocket and tried sticking the key into the lock, but my hand was shaking and I couldn't make it fit. I took another nip of brandy and that helped matters. I unlocked the door and stepped inside.

Slowly I walked through the darkened house, everything tidy and clean. Vacuumed floors, dusted windowsills, polished mirrors. Cleanliness next to godliness and so forth. I walked through the hallway

Factory Town

and came to the bedroom door. A light was flickering beneath the door, and I heard industrial music and carnal moans. For a long time I just stood there, thinking, thinking. Then I took a deep breath, shook the cobwebs from my brain, and pushed open the door.

A woman stood in the middle of the bedroom, swaying drunkenly, falling all over herself. Only it wasn't Piper Carver. It was the whore from the hotel. She wore a moth-eaten teddy, her breasts spilling out the top. Her lipstick was smeared, and heavy mascara did nothing to hide a pair of black eyes. Two men lay on the bed. One of them was a young man, enormously obese with a buzz cut, body completely shaved. The other man was old and skinny. The words Jesus Lives tattooed on his fingers. The pastor from the party. The young man was caressing the pastor's penis, but it remained small and shriveled. When the pastor saw me, he pushed the young man away and covered his body with an electric blanket. In the name of Jesus, he said, but he didn't finish his declaration.

The whore turned around. When she saw me, her eyes narrowed contemptuously into coin slots. You again! she said. What the fuck do you want?

Wh...what do I want? I stammered. This is my house! This is my bedroom.

Oh, please, she said. And then she walked over to the bed and sat on the fat man's semi-hard penis and started bouncing up and down, glaring at me with contempt.

Things got out of control in a hurry. I strode across the room and pulled the whore off the fat man, he pleading with me to let him come at least. Then I got right into her face and slapped her hard, staggering her. She released a high-pitched shriek and told me to stay away, stay away, but it was too late for that. A man can only take so much. I dragged her to the hardwood floor and pinned her arms above her head. Then I pulled my head back and jerked forward quickly, spearing the whore in the face. Blood spurted from her nose and spilled down her face and onto her chest.

The music stopped playing. I rose to my feet and the pastor and his companion watched in silence. The pastor reached into the nightstand drawer and pulled out a pipe and a Zippo lighter. He lit the pipe and sucked down the narcotic smoke, and soon his body went limp, his eyes rolling into the back of his head.

I towered over the whore, said, Serves you right, you goddamn whore. Charlie was right about you. Fucking the whole goddamn neighborhood. A goddamn shame. She moaned and groaned for a good long while before finally pulling herself to her feet. She glowered at me through bloodshot eyes and then staggered across the room, locating her leopard-skin purse. She fumbled through it for a while, tossing aside cigarette boxes and hypodermic needles and tampons and a diaphragm. She finally located her makeup kit. Without washing the blood from her nose and face, without tending to her cuts and bruises, she hastily began covering her face with foundation and concealer, blush and mascara. The end result was grotesque, an apocalyptic hooker.

I shook my head in disgust. Nothing but a god-

Factory Town

damn whore, I said.

Oh, go to hell, Russell.

I clenched my fists, ready to teach her a real lesson, but I resisted. Instead, I turned and walked out the door, kicking it shut behind me.

* * *

The keys to the hearse were in the ignition. Furtively, I glanced around the neighborhood. There wasn't another human being in sight. I opened the door and stepped into the driver's seat, then closed the door gently behind me. I hit the ignition and the engine grumbled for a few moments before catching. Then I drove.

I didn't know where I was going. Still, it felt good to be behind the wheel, to be the driver of the hearse, if not my destiny. The radio was tuned to a fire and brimstone preacher, and I listened to his voice but not the words. The sky was gray and, once again, it looked ready to rain or snow. Despite the fact that the heater was on full blast, I shivered as the car barreled down the avenue, lined with strip malls and car dealerships and fast food restaurants that seemed to repeat every few blocks.

I drove and drove, and eventually the suburbs were gone, and I found myself on an abandoned highway, the landscape changing to dirt and desolation. My windshield was cracked and blurry, the radio station going in and out and in again, mariachi music, the scariest thing I'd ever heard. And then up ahead I came upon a little strip with a post office and a liquor store and a bar, the neon sign flashing Budweiser, and me cold and hungry and lost.

I stepped out of the hearse, my legs weak and atrophied, and limped toward the bar, the sound of country music muted and blurry behind the door. I shoved open the door and it creaked, western movie-style. Inside there was a pool table with a game half-finished, some wooden booths and metal tables. The jukebox was playing, but the bar was empty, not even a bartender. I sat down at the counter and looked around, called out, but there was no answer. Minutes or hours passed, and I was impatient, angry, but then I heard a sickly voice behind me and I jumped. I spun around and saw an elderly man, ninety-years-old at least, wearing a newsboy's hat and a Boy Scout uniform, carrying a blind person's cane. He said: Sorry about that, mister. I didn't hear you come in. Hope you haven't been waiting too long. They say when you go blind your other senses become more acute. Not me. I'm seventy percent deaf, too. God piles it on, in my case.

It's no problem, I said.

Mike's the fellow who owns the place, but he had to run. Family emergency. His brother lost an arm in some farm machinery. Second arm he's lost. He told me to watch the place. I understand the irony. In any case, what can I get you?

I could use a beer, I said.

I can do that. Might take me just a minute...

The blind man felt his way around the counter and fumbled around the icebox for a beer. He found a Budweiser and cracked it open for me. Three bucks, he said. Cash only.

I slapped some green on the counter. There's five

Factory Town

dollars, I said. Keep the change.

Thank you, sir.

Course, it could be a single. You'd never know, would you?

He shook his head and smiled. No, sir. I guess I wouldn't.

I drank the beer and then another and another. Outside, the thunder groaned and a dog howled.

And then the door opened and in walked a man that I recognized, the last person I wanted to see. He had silver hair and a white suit stained with blood. Fennington, the Cowboy's secretary. As he entered, he didn't seem to notice me. He sat at the opposite end of the bar and tapped his fist a few times on the counter. C'mon, Paul, he said. I'm thirsty.

That you, Mr. Fennington?

In the flesh, Paul. Where's Mike?

Family emergency. Brother lost another arm.

Shame. Nice kid. Nice family. Well, what can you do? The devil makes you pay. Get me a drink, Paul. Fuzzy naval. And better make it a double.

The blind man fumbled around, touching each bottle as Fennington guided him toward the peach schnapps. He filled up a pint glass: 2/3 schnapps, 1/3 orange juice, stuck it in front of Fennington who quickly took to drinking. I remained in my seat, back turned slightly, sipping my own beer.

The bartender, Paul, sat down in a chair and stared straight ahead with his diseased eyes. After a while, I could hear him snoring lightly, although his eyes remained open, twitching.

I didn't dare glance down the bar counter. But soon I could feel Fennington's eyes boring through the back of my head. I finished my beer and wiped my mouth with the palm of my hand. And then the jukebox started playing, only it wasn't country music or super hits, it was a concerto, dark as hell, Sibelius or Tchaikovsky.

I heard footsteps. When I turned, I saw that Fennington had moved into the stool next to mine. He placed his hand on my shoulder. I figured I'd find you here, he said. Where the miserable go to hide.

I didn't say anything, just stared straight ahead.

How is the investigation going? Any luck in finding the girl?

I shook my head. No. No luck. I've made inquiries. Nobody knows anything, or, if they do, they won't tell me a thing. They'd just as soon let her die. And some people, the sheriff, the doctor, are placing obstacles in my way.

Well. They are misguided. And you should know that the Cowboy thanks you for your service. Thanks you for your commitment. He'd be happy to give you more money, if that's what it takes. A worthwhile investment, to be sure.

I rubbed my face with my hand. The music was loud, making it hard to think.

That won't help, I said. Ever since I arrived in this goddamn town, I've been lost. A series of darkened corridors, an endless number of riddles. I don't understand a thing, a goddamned thing!

Fennington took a long gulp from his fuzzy navel. Then he nodded his head slowly in a sign of empathy. Yes. Yes, indeed. Things are confusing, aren't they? But don't think too much. The answers will reveal themselves. All that matters is how things end.

Factory Town

We forget the rest.

This girl, this girl!

Perhaps if you read the *Book of Edicts*, things would become more comprehensible. Do you have a copy?

No. No, of course not.

For it is written: The town must die with us.

I've heard it before. I don't understand.

You should read the good book. Everything will be clear then.

But the girl...

Yes, the girl. She means everything and she means nothing.

Who is she?

Why, she's just a girl.

No. That can't be. Who...is...she? Who the fuck is she?

Please. Mr. Carver. Calm down.

I realized that I was now standing, face surely red with anger, and that I had knocked over my beer bottle, sending it shattering on the floor. The music had stopped playing, but Paul, the bartender, remained asleep or dead.

I need to know! I shouted. Who is the girl?

Yes. Well then. Mr. Carver. I shall tell you. This girl. Alana as you call her. She is the daughter of the Cowboy. Flesh and blood. So you see why it is so important—

You're lying!

No. I'm telling the truth.

Where is this cowboy? I'd like to pay him a visit. I'd like to discuss a few things.

That isn't possible, of course. The Cowboy is a

very busy man, indeed.

Too busy to chat with me, his potential murderer?

Please, Mr. Carver. You are out of control. Emotions are running high. Take a deep breath. We all want what is best for the girl. Isn't that right?

I don't know, I said. I just don't know.

Here, take this book. He handed me his copy of the *Book of Edicts*. Read it. That will make everything clear. The Cowboy isn't a bad man. Certainly not. He wants what is best for Alana. He wants what is best for Factory Town.

I dropped the book on the counter, shoved it aside. My father made a prophecy, I said. It's bound to come true! He knew the devil well. They were close confidants.

The Cowboy isn't a bad man. Your father isn't a bad man. Please listen to me!

I rose to my feet and staggered across the bar. Michael Fennington called after me, but I was done talking to him. I kicked open the front door and stood in the wind and the snow. I came upon the hearse, but it had been badly vandalized: wheels gone, windows shattered, steering wheel bent. I sat down on the ground, and I could feel hot tears rolling down my cheeks.

The town must die with us, I mumbled. We must die with the town.

I lay down, a weary man. I closed my eyes and soon I was asleep, drifting away from this wasteland that was now my home...

* * *

Factory Town

I awoke to the sounds of footsteps on the crumbling asphalt. I opened my eyes and saw a young boy, breathing heavily, racing down the sidewalk, his black cape swaying in the mist. The Annihilator.

CHAPTER 16

And so I followed after him. He was holding his toy sword and it was streaked with blood. He ran without slowing down, glancing stealthily over his shoulder every few minutes.

As I made my way down the shattered sidewalk, I noticed that my right leg was suddenly exceedingly sore, and it soon became very difficult for me to keep up the pace. With enormous exertion I would lunge forward, my leg dragging behind me uselessly, then lunge forward again, but as soon as I got within shouting distance the Annihilator would himself speed up and disappear into the night fog.

This went on for some time until I noticed we were back on the abandoned highway, the Annihilator racing down the middle of it, sword secure in its sheath, cape swaying majestically behind him. The black asphalt stretched ahead forever and I felt

Factory Town

scared, scared for the boy, scared for me.

The sound of thunder and gunfire off in the distance. And still the boy raced on. My head was aching, the wound worsening, my leg in bad shape as well, gangrene a distinct possibility.

And then I saw something that startled me. Up until this time the land surrounding the highway had been stark and vacant, nothing but snow-covered dirt and frozen sagebrush. But now I came to a small parcel of land illuminated by a gas lamp hanging from a poplar tree. And on the ground, flowers, hundred of them, all varieties and colors. Roses and daisies and lilies and tulips and poppies and on and on and on…

I sat down in the midst of the flowers and I felt a profound sadness; it had been so long since I'd seen any semblance of beauty. The cold wind blew and the moon was frozen. I closed my eyes and breathed deeply and then opened them again. Overwhelming color bathed in gas lamp light. I was overcome, and I had the strange notion to just stay there, stay there forever, because it was beautiful, and I knew it would always stay beautiful, while out there, back on the highway, back in Factory Town, it would remain ugly and terrible, monsters hiding behind bushes, ready to pounce. But I had promises to keep, so I got down on all fours and began picking the flowers, picking them by handfuls, and then stuffing them in my pockets. I stayed on the ground for a long time, and then I noticed that I was crying, tears of pain, tears of regret, and when I rose to my feet I was covered with the petals of a China Rose. I wiped the petals from my clothes, wiped the tears from my eyes, and then I got back on the highway.

Jon Bassoff

* * *

Somehow, despite my detour, the boy remained within sight. I limped along, pockets full of flowers, and eventually the boy veered off the highway and onto a dirt road, turned muddy. I shouted out, but he didn't turn back, and the only light was the moon shining through the thick clouds. I was gasping for breath and my head was aching and my leg was dying. And then the stark terrain gave way to some trees, and at first there were just a few of them scattered across the plains, but the farther we walked the more dense the trees became until we were in a forest, dark and cold.

The branches and brambles tore my skin, and I tried desperately to keep up with the boy, but the woods were thick, and I kept stumbling and falling, and finally I gave up and sat down on a rock, and never before had the night been so dark and the wind so cold and the trees so menacing.

And then I heard the sound of leaves crunching. My eyes gazed toward where I heard the noise, but all was darkness. I held my breath, fearful of an animal or something worse. For the next several minutes all was quiet. But then I heard the sound again. I groaned, and it was the groan of terror.

I heard a voice, that of an old woman. My precious, my precious.

I rose to my feet, swung around, eyes wild, and whispered: Who's there?

No answer. Silence. The wind stopped blowing. Everything was still.

Factory Town

And then, after several minutes of agony, the voice again: Where'd you bury 'em? You can tell me. I have secrets, too.

Come out! Show your face!

More rustling, more darkness. I took a step forward and removed my sword from the hilt. I could feel my heart pounding in my chest. I needed to make it home through the forest. I know you're there, I said.

The frozen moon broke through the mist, and then she was directly in front of me, her hair white and wild, her skin pale. She grinned a terrible grin and said, I've been waiting for you, precious, and showed me a gunny sack, and inside there were children, children she'd taken from beds and playgrounds, and I panicked, started swinging my sword wildly, and I got a piece of her shoulder, staggering her backwards, and then I was running, running through the forest with Ms. Marcell, the hunchback, on my heels.

I ran forever with my cape whipping in the cold, mean wind, and the evil woman kept after me, telling me about the quilt she'd made out of children's skin, and I'd heard stories, so many terrible stories, and then I was in a familiar neighborhood all filled with one-story brick ranches, and she was gone, and I walked slowly down the street, and I heard the distant sound of a train horn, muted and blurry. My heart was pounding, my body trembling. I wanted to stop, wanted to sleep, but it was too late for that, so I continued through a frozen dirt field and along a little gully until I saw a darkened farmhouse surrounded by a collapsed picket fence, and this is where the party had been.

Jon Bassoff

I walked up the porch steps, tightening the cape around my neck. The front door was open a crack, and I pushed it open and stepped inside. The lights were all turned off, and everything was dark. I walked slowly through the living room, the hardwood floor creaking beneath my feet. I had almost made it to the stairs when a light flashed on. A woman sat on the couch, eyes bloodshot, hair wild. It was Nicole, the woman who'd been beaten so badly by her husband. Her lipstick and mascara were smeared across her face grotesquely. There was a nearly empty bottle of red wine, shot dead, bleeding on the floor. She spoke, her voice harsh. Where have you been, little boy?

I didn't say a word, just stood there staring at her.

I said, where have you been?

Walking, I said.

She smiled but it was the saddest smile I'd ever seen. Walking. That's fine. And with that cape, always with that cape. You gonna save the world?

I shrugged my shoulders.

Sure you are. The Annihilator. But you gotta save yourself first, don't you know it?

I nodded my head. Yes, ma'am.

She laughed. Smart boy, she said. And then she motioned me toward her, and I edged over slowly, cautiously, glancing toward the front door, afraid that he would soon crash into the living room, and then there would be hell to pay.

She grabbed my wrist and pulled me toward her face. I could smell the gin and cigarettes on her breath. That fellow, she said, he's a mean one, ain't he? Does some awful things to the both of us.

Yes, ma'am.

Factory Town

He gets jealous. Sometimes he drinks too much. It ain't his fault, Russell. Nothing is nobody's fault.

I didn't say anything, just shook my head.

I guess I shouldn't have married him, knowing what I know now. But he used to be a nice boy, just like you. He used to bring me a white rose every Friday night. A single white rose. Yes, Russell. He was the first boy that ever loved me.

And then her eyes got all crazy-like, and she started biting down on her lower lip until blood was spurting out, and that made me scared. I could feel hot tears filling up my eyes. I backed away from her and made my way to the staircase, barely breathing at all.

Where you going, boy? Where you going? Please. Don't leave me like this. I'm begging you. You don't know what he's bound to do. He's a monster. A shot to the head or a knife to the throat is too humane for the bastard. Come back, Russell. Please...

But I never turned back.

And now upstairs, I walked down the long hallway lined with photographs of smiling faces and happiness, a grotesque misrepresentation of the past. I could still hear Nicole's voice echoing across the hallway—don't leave me like this—and then I came to a familiar room, the sign on the door reading, *The Annihilator Waits Here*. I took a deep breath, my throat constricted from anxiety. I opened the door and stepped inside.

Everything was the same, the way it had always been. Posters of superheroes on the walls. Toys and action figures scattered across the floor. I closed my eyes and listened to the pounding of my own heart.

Jon Bassoff

I took off my cape and my mask, dropped my sword to the floor, and removed my clothes. I turned out the light and got into bed and pulled the covers over my body. I stared at the ceiling, and I thought about terrible things, always terrible things.

* * *

Hours passed and then that man Cory Packer stood in the doorway of my room, the naked light bulb swinging behind him, his shadow lengthening and shortening and lengthening again on the hardwood floor. I was awake, heart beating rapidly, sweat covering my brow, but I pretended like I was asleep because I knew he'd been drinking; he'd always been drinking. He took a few steps into my room and I squeezed my eyes tight, tried to travel to another world. I could hear him muttering under his breath, talking about his goddamn worthless wife and his goddamn worthless son and his goddamn worthless job, and then he stopped talking and I could hear him breathing, the slow labored breathing of a drunk.

Get out of bed, you little piece of shit, he said, and I squeezed my eyes tighter. But he wouldn't let it go—he was a relentless drunk—and I could hear the floor creaking beneath the shifting of his feet. Then he stood over me, and I felt the tears welling in my eyes, always the coward. Always the coward! he said, as he pulled me to my feet.

He looked at me, and there was madness in his eyes. He said: Listen to me, Russell, listen to me good! You think you're better than me? Well, do you? Fuck you, little boy. You ain't shit. You look at me

Factory Town

like I'm some goddamn monster. I see it in your eyes. Like I'm a goddamn monster. But it ain't my fault. I was wired that way. Genetics. My old man, he was the same way. And his old man before. It's a history of rage, a history of hate. And you ain't no different. No, sir. I'll make a prophecy, and forgive me if I ain't the religious kind. And the prophecy is this: you'll do bad. You hear me? You'll do bad! Worse than me even! But it all ain't bad, boy. You'll own this place some day. Own the abandoned buildings and abandoned storefronts, own the decaying houses and the decaying neighborhoods, own the hateful men and the despondent women, own the wind and the trash and the dirt.

I nodded my head, I don't know why, and then the old man let me have it, and it was just for kicks for him. He pinned me down on the floor and took to hitting me, backhands and forehands, and my nose and ears filled with blood, and I closed my eyes and imagined that I was far, far away...

...and then he was done with me, and he staggered out of my room leaving me bloody and battered and begging for mercy, but he forgot his prized cowboy hat, left it lying on the floor.

* * *

I ate breakfast with the woman — Cheerios for me, only water for her — and neither of us spoke, but she eyed me funny; she knew what had happened the night before, but she was too scared to do anything about it.

That man still sleeping? I finally asked, and she

Jon Bassoff

seemed shocked by the question.

Why, yes, she said. He works very hard. At the factory. It's a thankless job, Russell.

And that was that. I ate my Cheerios, and the woman drank her water, and for a long time neither one of us talked. When she did speak, her voice sounded different, and it scared me.

She said: Sometimes I sit on that front porch for hours at a time, staring down that long road, waiting for a car or a truck or a motorcycle to appear to take me away, but when one does come, I don't move a muscle, I just sit there and watch as it pulls away, the taillights becoming smaller and smaller and finally being swallowed into the night. And I keep a flask of bourbon beneath the wicker chair, just a nip now and then to dull my senses, to warm my frigid skin. And when I see Corey's shadow, when I hear Corey's footsteps, when I sense Corey's presence — those are the moments when I drink more than a nip; those are the moments when I tilt the flask a little steeper...

CHAPTER 17

Later, I sat outside the house, hiding behind a rusted and abandoned mail truck. Crows and bats flew overhead. The sun was beginning to rise over the plains, and the sky was a bloody mess. The ground was still covered with snow, filthy most of it. Piano music played from a distant house, sad and haunting. I blew on my hands, trying to keep them warm. The bandage on my head had come loose, and blood was falling to the snow like a dripping faucet.

And then way off in the distance the factory whistle blew, and moments later the front door opened, and Cory Packer stood on the porch wearing a flannel shirt and blue jeans and those cowboy boots and cowboy hat. He gazed off into the distance and squinted in the early light. In his right hand he clutched a metal lunch bucket; in his left hand a thermos.

Jon Bassoff

He walked slowly through the neighborhood, with his head down, kicking at the sidewalk angrily, spitting from time to time. Singing a song, under his breath, an angry tune:

We dig dig dig dig dig dig dig in our mine the whole day through
To dig dig dig dig dig dig dig is what we really like to do
It ain't no trick to get rich quick
If you dig dig dig with a shovel or a pick
In a mine! In a mine! In a mine! In a mine!
Where a million diamonds shine!

And after a while, other workers joined him for the march, appearing from inside brick houses and wood shacks and from behind trees. They all wore blue jumpsuits and yellow hardhats, and none of them spoke to each other or even made eye contact. Many of the workers were badly maimed or deformed: missing legs and arms, scarred faces and necks. It was a strange sight to be sure, a group of fifty at least, limping and staggering through the neighborhoods and toward the factory with its strange goings-on.

Once they approached the town center, once they could see the steam billowing sinisterly from the smokestacks, Cory Packer began singing again, and the rest of the workers joined him for the chorus:

Heigh-ho, heigh-ho
It's off to work we go
We keep on singing all day long

Factory Town

Heigh-ho

The factory towered over the town, eight stories at least, smokestacks even taller, gray brick walls covered with steel catwalks and darkened windows, many of them shattered. And surrounding the property, barbed wire fencing, half-buried in rubble and drifts of snow.

The men marched onward, heads down, knees high, and I watched from a distance, curious about this place and these people. What were they making in there? What did they make for ghosts?

From behind the gates, a man appeared with tomato-red hair and a lime-green suit, and he stared at his watch, arm raised delaying entrance, and the workers waited patiently, still singing their song, but quieter now, and then the man lowered his hand and the whistle blew, and the door opened, and the workers marched in, a sea of blue and yellow.

I remained across the street, waiting, suddenly anxious, maybe even frightened. There were problems, of course, so many problems, but answers often make things worse, truth often destroys. I buried my hands in my pockets and crossed the street, the wind blowing cold and mean.

I got into line behind the last of the workers, but when it was finally my turn to enter, the man with the green suit simply shook his head. This is a private building, he said. No trespassers.

There's somebody I need to see.

I'm sorry. No trespassers.

Then perhaps you could tell me. What goes on in there? What are they producing? It's not like any factory I've ever seen.

You don't belong here. I demand you leave or I will call the sheriff. He doesn't like outsiders, hear? And neither do I.

I was about to argue some more when something caught my eye, a furtive movement fifty or so yards down the fence. Mumbling a farewell, I wandered along the perimeter, the barbed wire tearing my clothes and cutting my arms. The factory whistle blew again.

My legs weren't working well, but eventually I arrived to the area along the fence where I had seen the movement. Pulling herself through a snowdrift, her leg stumps dragging uselessly behind, shivering badly, body bloody and emaciated, brown eyes sunken and resigned. Charlie's mother. She wore the same white nightgown, and her skin was pale and beginning to slough off her face. Our eyes met, and she blinked a few times, nothing more. Mrs. Gardner? I said. What are you doing here? Are you lost? Did somebody leave you here? She shook her head and tried speaking, but I heard only deathly wheezing. I leaned in closer. I can't hear you, I said. What are you saying?

She tried again, this time with enormous effort. Escaping…this…town.

And then she closed her eyes. Without thinking, I scooped up the old woman in my arms and started walking. It's gonna be okay, I whispered to her. We've gotta get you cleaned up. We've gotta get you some food and water. Hang in there, you hear me?

The sky was gray and dark, ominous as hell. I held the dying woman in my arms and walked through

Factory Town

the town, searching for aid, searching for food.

People passed me on the streets, but nobody looked up, nobody made eye contact, despite my pleading, despite my shouting. Finally, I got the attention of a young man wearing a Himalayan hat. He had a kind face, although psychotic eyes. Please, sir, I said. I need your help. This woman will die if she doesn't eat or drink soon. Can you help? But he pushed right past me, and as he did so, he stabbed me in the side with some sort of a shiv. I coughed in pain, but continued moving.

Mrs. Gardner was breathing, but barely, her dying eyes focused on mine. I stroked her head, her belly, and she moaned softly.

I approached a woman with wild red hair, wearing a tattered fur coat. I said: Please help me, ma'am, I don't know who to turn to. This woman, Mrs. Gardner, she hasn't eaten in some time. She'll starve to death. Please help. The woman looked at me and then at Mrs. Gardner. Suddenly her face took on an expression of complete and absolute terror. She got right into my face and started screaming hysterically and belligerently. She pounded her head with her hand and bit her lip until it was bleeding. As for me, I got the hell away from the woman, and I knew time was running out for Charlie's mother, for Alana, for me.

The sky was gray and the snow was dirty. All around me was desolation and corrosion. I started running, and the old woman stared at me with those sad eyes, but not for much longer. I held her hand and it felt like a too-ripe peach. Her hair was all but gone now, and I could feel her ribs pressing against her skin.

I came to a set of cement stairs, going down, down, down, always down. I was curious, so I gripped Mrs. Gardner tighter and descended. The stairs were steep and seemed to go on forever. I thought I heard footsteps behind me, but every time I looked back, the stairs were empty. Up above lightning flashed, no thunder.

Finally I came to the bottom of the gray stairway. There was a cement square, maybe ten by ten feet. On the square, six inches or so of water. All sorts of junk floated in the water: an empty can of beans, a hypodermic needle, a necktie, a rusted knife, a rosary. And, most interestingly, four or five cutthroat trout, swimming below the surface, their silver stomachs dragging against the cement.

I knew what I had to do. Gently, I placed Mrs. Gardner on one of the lower steps. She curled into the fetus position, her breath slow and labored. I stepped into the water, which came up to my ankles. I kept my eye on one of the trout, the one that appeared the most lethargic. I waited until it swam up to my foot and then reached down to grab it. Despite its lethargy, it managed to dart away. I took a few more steps in, took a few deep breaths, and snatched at it again. I was quicker this time and managed to grab a hold of it for a moment before it slipped out of my hands and fell back into the water, swimming away spastically.

This went on for a long time, numerous attempts and numerous failures, until finally I caught him. He was a decent-sized fella, maybe eight inches in length. He flipped wildly, and I squeezed him tightly until his skin began to burst. Then I brought him over

Factory Town

to the stairs and slammed him against the cement until he was still.

I grabbed the rusted knife from the water. I held the trout around the middle with its underbelly facing me. Methodically, I inserted the knife into the anus and removed the gill cavity and entrails. Then I grabbed his head and snapped it back before finally yanking off the skin.

Cautiously, I approached the old woman. I placed the skinned fish in front of her face. She raised her head, regarded it for a few moments, then lay her head back on the cement. C'mon, ma'am, I said. You gotta eat. Otherwise you'll die.

I tore off a piece of flesh and tried pushing it into her mouth, but she shook her head and closed her mouth tightly.

Goddamn it! C'mon!

But it was no use. The woman had given up, her eyes full of pain and resignation. So I sat with her as the sky turned from gray to black and the snow fell on the living and the dead. I sang old Irish folk songs I had learned from my grandmother, and Mrs. Gardner listened, her weary head resting on my lap. I was consumed by an overwhelming sadness. I prayed to a God that never existed that she would die quickly; such pain is unbearable. And then, as the soft snow covered our bodies, Mrs. Gardner closed her eyes, her body relaxed, and she was gone.

With trembling hands, I reached into my pockets and pulled out a couple of Indian Head pennies. I placed the pennies on the woman's eyes, a fare for Charon.

Jon Bassoff

I sat there for a long time, holding the still-warm body to my chest. I started crying, and it was for all of the things I'd lost and all of the things I'd never had. This place, Factory Town, was filled with such misery and grief, and I feared that I was stuck here for eternity, a punishment for sins that were preordained.

And then I heard footsteps, loud and monotonous, and a light shone down from the top of the staircase. I shielded my eyes with my hand. Cory Packer stood there, the light behind him, his face in the shadows, his body as still as an effigy.

CHAPTER 18

And then I was in the darkness, lying on my back, birth naked, my ears filled with the sounds of tortured screams and dripping water. I squeezed my eyes shut, tried to forget. Charlie's mother was dead and my hands were trembling.

I rose to my feet, waiting for my eyes to adjust, but the blackness remained. I felt around with my hands. Four walls of cement, cold. No door, no opening. Nothing left for me to do but shout. So I shouted. I shouted with all my might, shouted until I thought my chest would explode. But no sounds came from my mouth. Suddenly I was a mute...

...and an asylum patient. I ran back and forth across the enclosure, pounding my fists against the wall, yanking out my hair by the clumps, biting chunks of my own flesh.

Still darkness, only darkness.

Jon Bassoff

I was alone. Completely and utterly alone. But no, that can never be the case. My own mind, my own thoughts haunted me. In a strange car, driving down an endless dirt road overtaken by weeds and fallen trees and dead animals (coyotes and raccoons and owls and cattle), going farther and farther down that road and further and further away from sanity. Soon the road disappears and the windshield starts moving. It's covered with moths, thousands of them, crawling, flapping their wings spastically. And then up ahead appears a brilliant light and it is a bush all lit on fire, but there is no angel, there is no God of Abraham. The moths are attracted to the light and fly away from the car, flutter into the fire, all of them, a holocaust of choice. I step out of the car, away from the fire, and I hear the moaning of a thousand voices or more, a purgatory choir. I stumble through the woods, branches and brambles tearing my skin, fires all around me, trees and mining cabins and animals engulfed, alarms ringing like the devil screaming from his throne. Then my right hand is gripping a shovel, and I'm digging, digging, digging, a grave for somebody. I toss the shovel aside and keep walking and come upon a hatch all covered with branches and brambles. I pull open the hatch and am staring at my own face covered with leeches and ants and flies...

    I screamed, and now I could no longer tell the difference between fantasy and reality, between nightmares and wakefulness. How long had I been here? In this darkness? In Factory Town? I stuck my hands in my pockets. The flowers that I'd picked so long ago were still there. I pulled out a handful, stuck them to my nose, and breathed deeply. There was still some beauty left, even here in this wretchedness. And then I thought of Alana. I squeezed my eyes shut and tried remembering her face, but I couldn't. She'd vanished...

Time passed, time passed. I heard voices but they sounded strange, otherworldly. I jumped to my feet and, voice returning, shouted out with new vigor: Hey! Hey! I'm in here! Help me! I'm in here! The voices got louder and louder, although still muted, blurry. And then the sound of footsteps. I shouted some more, my heart pounding in my ribcage. Then the footsteps stopped and the voices faded away. I was heartbroken and terrified. What if I were in this blackness forever? What if I were buried alive?

It was too terrible to think about.

I began shouting again, but the footsteps and voices didn't return. So I began wishing for death.

And then the lights switched on. I was now inside some sort of a small interrogation room. And standing in the corner, leaning against the wall, was a man dressed all in camouflage. He had a gray goatee and his head was shaved bald. His face was pale, his eyes those of a lunatic. Had he been standing there this whole time?

I shook my head in fright. What the hell is going on? I said. Who are you? Where am I? What am I doing here?

The man took a few steps forward and stuck out his hand, a gesture which went unreciprocated. Mr. Carver, he said. My name is Timothy Kaladi. I'm sorry to have startled you in that way.

What do you want? Why am I trapped here?

I'm here to help, he said. I'm here to provide answers.

Answers? To what questions?

He smiled. About Alana. Naturally.

My head was spinning, and I feared for my own sanity. I worried that this man, Timothy Kaladi, was a figment of my diseased mind. And then I decided that it didn't matter, that this world was nothing more than an overturned piss-pot.

I sat down in the corner and started rocking back and forth. Kaladi remained leaning against the wall, studying me the way a psychiatrist would study a patient. And perhaps that's what I was.

You should know, he said, that we believe she is alive and well. Although certainly in great danger.

Where is she? I said, voice cracking badly.

That I can't tell you. But we have some leads. And as soon as we find her we will put her in a secure location and you won't have to worry about a thing...

I don't understand. I don't understand anything.

You met the Cowboy's secretary, I understand? Mr. Fennington?

Yes.

And he wanted your help in finding her?

Yes. He paid me. And he said there'd be more once I found her.

Yes. Of course. And he will pay you. He's a man of his word.

He kept talking about something called the *Book of Edicts*.

Kaladi nodded his head. Of course he did. He's a fundamentalist. A true believer.

Well? What's it all about?

Factory Town

The Holy Book for Factory Town. The new vision, as seen by the Cowboy.

A new vision? I still don't understand. How does this relate to Alana?

Not just Alana. All children.

All children? But what...

I should come clean, Mr. Carver. About myself. About my past. You see, I've done some terrible things. Things I'm not proud of. He grinned quickly, but then his face took on a pained expression, his lower lip trembling, as if he were going to break down and sob. And yet, when he spoke his voice was seemingly void of emotion. It all started, I guess, with a girl in Cheyenne. Name of Rosa. Absolutely gorgeous. I saw her a few times working at a diner. I never talked to her even though I wanted to. This one night, I followed her home along the railroad track. The moon was full, Mr. Carver, and I was good and wild! I waited until the train whistle blew, and then I came up from behind and grabbed her, and she screamed, and I dragged her into a ditch. I raped her there. I might have killed her, but I can't say for certain. She was breathing when I left...

There was another girl in Denver. Terrible flirt. She sat on my lap before I'd even said a word to her. I charmed her and took her to a rundown hotel with broken mirrors and a broken bedframe. I raped her, too. I can't even tell you why. I was full of rage in those days. When I got done with her, her face was all bruised and bloody and swollen, and she was crying. She was a flirt, but she didn't deserve that. I see that now.

There were other girls, he said. One in Topeka,

one in Des Moines, one outside of Dallas. And then I got reckless. Got into a little jam. Ended up killing a man in Jackson. Not entirely accidental. Sliced his neck with a Bowie knife. Terrible mess. And that's why, that's how, I ended up here.

Here?

In Factory Town. It's where all of us are sent. One way or another.

Why are you telling me this? About your past?

Because I'm no angel. I want you to know that. I'm a sinner just like everybody else. I'm not trying to be sanctimonious. I can't afford to be.

I was getting frustrated. Kaladi talked about answers, but he was only providing more questions, more confusion. The *Book of Edicts*, I said. You were talking about the *Book of Edicts*.

Ah, yes. The mythological story of our town. Warm Springs Asylum and William Farley and so on and so on.

A nun told me the story, I said. How Farley started a factory and needed workers so he pilfered from the asylum. How they rebelled and butchered Farley and damn near everybody in town. How the remaining lunatics stayed back and started Factory Town.

Kaladi laughed. Yes, that's the story. The way some create meaning.

You don't buy it?

It doesn't matter if I buy it or not. What does matter is that a whole lot of people do believe in it, and they are ready to take the next step.

Which is?

Haven't you heard the mantra, Mr. Carver?

Mantra?

Factory Town

Certainly. The final conclusion of the *Book of Edicts*. *The town must die with us.*

Yes, I said. I've heard it. But I don't understand.

Too much misery, the Cowboy says. Too much sin. Hard to argue with him.

And?

We can't escape our fate. We are degenerates, rapists, murderers, pedophiles. And we all live here together in this little town. Eventually we'll die out, naturally. But there'll be a new generation. And the Cowboy fears that they will repeat the sins of their fathers, the sins of their mothers. And this can't happen. So...

No children, I interrupted. No children at all.

Precisely. The most important decree: No child shall be born alive in this town.

Thus the importance of Dr. Byrd.

Yes. The abortionist.

But Alana?

There have been some dissidents. A handful at least. I include myself as one of them. And we started an underground railroad of sorts. Saving a few live born babies. Hiding them from the Cowboy and his followers. Only a handful have survived. Alana is one of them. But she's missing.

So the Cowboy, he —

Yes. Kills them. Disposes of the bodies. Continues his aim of turning Factory Town into a ghost town, thus ending the cycle of sin. He thinks himself noble, of course. Most delusional men do.

And that's why I was sent here. To find her.

Kaladi rubbed his face with his hand. No, he said. That's wrong.

Jon Bassoff

What the hell are you talking about?

And now he spoke in a hushed voice. What you should know, he said, is that we all need a narrative to rely on. Especially when the walls have come crashing down. Especially when we're nearly out of time...

Stop! You're speaking in code! You're—

Your temple, he interrupted. It's bleeding very badly. This much is obvious: you don't have long to live, my friend.

It was at that moment that I heard terrible noises, unbearable. High pitch shrieks. Fingernails scraping on cement. Threats whispered in my ears. And then the walls around me started crumbling down, broke apart by graveyard shovels. Frantic screaming, most likely from me. Moments passed, terrible moments, and I was surrounded by a group of men, brandishing shovels and knives and hammers, all wearing black suits and gas masks.

CHAPTER 19

I thought I was a goner for sure, with the way the blood was pouring down my face, with the way these menacing men surrounded me. These were the Cowboy's men, I was certain about that, and they moved forward en mass, a frightening sight. Fearing for my life, I fell to the floor and closed my eyes and shielded my head. I could hear their voices, muffled beneath their gasmasks, chanting the same phrase over and over again: The town must die with us. The town must die with us. The town must die with us.

And then I felt one of the men grab a hold of my body and try to flip me to my back, but I resisted, kicking and flailing and spitting. Soon more of the men came to his aid. It took several of them, and it took a good long while, but eventually they got me immobilized, arms and legs spread-eagle. My ligaments were being stretched, my tendons ruptured, and I shrieked in pain. One of the men—they all looked identical in their suits and masks—stood over me, his eyes nothing but slits, and removed several long silver nails from his suit pocket. His breathing became heavier and heavier, and he got down to his knees and proceeded to place one of the nails on the palm of my hand, drawing blood. I knew what would come next and I screamed in panic. The masked man raised the hammer high in the air and I squeezed my eyes shut...

Then I heard a voice boom behind me: Gentlemen, I command you to cease! Stop this brutality at once! This man is not an enemy. He is a trusted employee.

Cautiously I opened my eyes. The hammer remained high in the air, frozen. Glancing past the masked man's shoulder, I saw Michael Fennington with his stained white suit, his gray hair slicked back impeccably. Drop the hammer! he shouted. At this very moment! He seemed to have a certain authority with these men, and immediately they released me, the hammer and nails clanging harmlessly to the floor.

Still unnerved, I pulled myself to all fours and scampered up against the wall. I was having difficulty breathing, screeches sounding with each inhalation. Fennington approached me, a good-natured smile on his face, and shook his head. My dear sir, he said. That must have been a harrowing experience. I must apologize for their behavior. They are an excitable bunch. But they mean no harm. They are only trying to do the will of the Cowboy.

I regained my breath. They...they were going to kill me. A crucifixion of the innocent.

Factory Town

Yes, indeed, indeed. A terrible violation. And yet you are still living, thank the good Lord for that! But enough of that. I must ask you: is there any word about the girl, Alana? Any progress in her recovery?

I sat there for a moment, still stunned, unable to respond. Then, slowly, I nodded my head. Yes, I said. I'm getting close. I'm sure of it.

That's wonderful! Thrilling! And have you had a chance to read the decrees? Do you understand why she is so important to the Cowboy?

Yes, I said. I understand.

He reached into his pocket and pulled out a wad of cash, dropped it on my lap. More money, he said. For your hard work.

I shoved it away. This money is worthless, I said. I know that now.

Fennington grinned. Worthless? Not at all. We have the power to assign worth. To money. To life. There is great value, I believe, in both. In any case, we'll be in touch, Mr. Carver.

And with that he turned and walked away, through the rubble, into the darkness, his masked men following directly behind.

* * *

Back outside, back in the town center, there was more pandemonium, another wave of suicides, this time self-immolations, a dozen or more people on fire, faces melting from their skulls.

I watched from a distance, but with great interest, while the rest of the townsfolk didn't seem to notice, didn't seem to care. There were no cries of terror, no attempts to extinguish the fires, no shielding their eyes from the grotesqueness of it all.

And then Charlie Gardner, my childhood friend, was standing next to me, shaking his head, saying, Terrible things are happening here. *Either there is a civil strife in heaven, or else the world, too saucy with the gods, incenses them to send destruction.* It's a wonder I don't leave. It's a wonder everybody doesn't leave.

Your mother...

I know. A shame. But she spent her last moments with you. For that we should be thankful, don't you think?

So we walked along, doing our best to ignore the blood curdling screams all around us. Money was falling from my pocket, scattering on the ground. It was night again. It was always night. Crows flew overhead, but they were outmatched. The Vultures stood at the ready. And where was God? Hanging from a noose.

The factory, I said. They wouldn't let me in to the factory.

Charlie shrugged his shoulders, said, There's nothing to see there. Nothing at all. It's just a factory.

No. No, I don't believe that.

But your imagination, Russell. It's becoming your reality. That's dangerous, good buddy!

Then take me there. Take me inside the factory. I want to see for myself.

Charlie shook his head. That would be difficult, I'm afraid. Very difficult indeed.

Why? What are they trying to hide in there?

Hide? Nothing. It's just a matter of clearance. Security reasons and such. You see, the Cowboy, he—

Factory Town

The Cowboy! He has the answers. Take me to him. I want to meet him. I want to talk to him.

Charlie laughed a deep guttural laugh. Russell Carver, you really are too much!

This is madness, I said, and he seems to be in charge of it all. I want to talk to him.

But that is hardly possible.

What is it with you? Aren't you going to help me? Isn't anybody going to help me? Are you content to just stand by and watch as sin breeds like mosquitoes in a marsh? Are you content to just stand by and watch humanity crumble like your abandoned buildings?

More laughter. Such poetry, he said. And certainly I am not content. But I am resigned. You want to see the Cowboy? Well then, Russell. You will see him. But nothing will change. Your words will not move him, no matter how poetic they are. And this detour will only distract you from locating the girl, whatever girl you are looking for. It's a shame about Alana. It's a shame about my mother.

I bowed my head, the tears welling in my eyes.

But we will go see the Cowboy. Surely you will be disappointed.

So I waited for him to lead, but instead Charlie stopped walking and crossed his arms.

Well? I said. Which way do we go?

You tell me. You know the way.

I shook my head. That's ridiculous. I've never seen him before in my life. I've never seen any of you before in my life.

Start walking, Russell. You'll find him. I'll be right behind you. I'll let you know if you've taken a wrong

Jon Bassoff

turn. But you won't. You know the way.

And so...and so...I walked. I walked through the streets and there was no rhyme or reason to where I was going, and Charlie remained behind me, ten yards back, grinning like a fool, a yellow cigarette dangling from his mouth, unlit. The sky was black; this was the longest night yet. Off in the distance I could hear the popping of fireworks. Away from the town's center I walked, through a snow-covered field, Charlie not saying a word.

We can't live without light, we can't live without sleep, and there was rustling behind bushes and trees, eyes shining grotesquely in the darkness. The popping of the fireworks became louder, and it was in that direction I was drawn. The air became thick with smoke, smoke from the fireworks, and soon I was coughing, eyes stinging badly.

I came across a group of men, skin the color of charcoal, safety goggles covering their eyes. They were huddled in a circle lighting off aerial shells and firecrackers and flying spinners and roman candles and sparklers. You take beauty where you can find it. The flowers were still in my pockets.

When the men saw me, they panicked. One of them said something in a language I didn't recognize, and then the rest of them began shoveling away dirt and snow with their hands, looking to create a pit to hide their fireworks. It didn't matter that I was standing right in front of them watching them with my very eyes; they dug frantically, tossed the fireworks in the shallow hole, and quickly covered it again with dirt and snow. But what did they use the fireworks for? Entertainment? A signal for help?

Factory Town

I watched with confusion as they carried on for another fifteen minutes at least, burying their fireworks the way that a squirrel buries nuts. I glanced behind me, looked for Charlie, but he'd vanished again as was often the case with him.

Slowly, I took a few steps forward, and one of the men rose to his feet and waved his hands frantically. It's okay, I said, but they were all in a panic, sitting on their haunches, eyes wide and wild. It's okay, I said again, but they seemed to be foreigners, unfamiliar with my language.

I studied them for a few moments. They were dressed oddly, as if they'd raided the bargain bin at a ramshackle department store, clothes outsized or terribly small, shoes mismatched or missing completely. I could tell that they scared easily, so I raised my hands plaintively and took another few steps forward. A few of them leaned backward, raising hands above their eyes as if they were shielding themselves from the devil himself.

I'm not going to hurt you, I said. I'm lost, you see. I'm looking for a man. He calls himself the Cowboy. El Vaquero. Can you help me? Do any of you understand?

There was a general murmuring among the men, but none of them responded to my questions. As I studied them further, I noticed that their faces were identical. All eight of them. Octuplets.

And so we stayed like that for some time, measuring each other. It seemed to me that I'd been wandering in circles forever, and I was unsure of everything that I'd ever known. There was no way out, that much I knew, and yet I fought for a reason to believe, and that was the most terrible thing of all.

Time passed forever, and then one of the men rose slowly, squinting his eyes in the darkness. I can talk with you, he said with an unfamiliar accent.

That's good. I—

You should know we been watching you. From distance.

Watching me?

Yes, yes. But what you want? What you looking for?

The Cowboy, I said. Where is he?

The Cowboy?

Yes.

He gone.

What?

Gone. And he motioned with his hands, a fluttering bird to the sky.

I shook my head. You're wrong, I said. He's not gone. He runs this town with an iron fist.

No. Gone.

Angry and frustrated, I turned my back on the strange men and started walking in the direction from which I'd come. But I hadn't walked more than a half dozen steps when I heard a trilling whistle. I turned around. Each of the octoplets now had a hand raised, pointing vaguely in the opposite direction. I jerked my head and, up ahead, saw the factory, smoke billowing from the stacks, the rain now suddenly changing to snow.

CHAPTER 20

The sky was dark, but intermittent lightning created a strobe-light effect, disconcerting as hell. I smoothed back my hair with blood and then continued on toward the factory, the gate now wide open, security missing.

The factory building was dark and menacing and towered above the grounds, which were all covered with rubble and wrecked machinery and crushed helmets and death, death, death, and along the way I met people, grotesque all, including, but not limited to: an old woman wearing a wedding dress from long ago, steely gray hair cascading down her back, pool blue eyes haunted, mouth open wide, hands bloody; a well-dressed man with round spectacles and a neatly trimmed goatee, a pocket watch in one hand and a derringer in the other; a crippled woman wearing the mask of a china doll, her left arm withered away; a dwarf of a man carrying a calico cat, its ears and eyes missing, hissing terribly; an obese woman, six hundred pounds at least, lapping up vomit from a wooden pail; Siamese twins, connected at the head, singing a song while banging their hands against the wall: *I went to see my boy in his room, I killed him and used his head for a broom*; an impossibly skinny man, his hair shaved revealing a lobotomy scar, his eyes dull and unblinking; a woman wearing stockings and nothing more, nose and mouth covered with blood, eyes pecked out by crows; a man dressed as a clown, head severed and lying several feet away, mouth still painted into a grin; an elderly ship captain with a long beard all soaked through with blood, flesh blackening and stinking of decay; and finally, Miguel Romero, the Messiah, the last hope for salvation, bowler's hat in hand, eyes bugging out, body hanging from a skeletal oak tree...

These people I saw and more, and I heard a voice whispering in my ear, They're insane, clearly they're insane. And you're one of them, mister. Don't you get it? This is Factory Town!

I closed my eyes and heard strange noises, faraway: the ghostly static of a radio, the howling of a wounded dog, the muted music of a calliope. I tried my best to remember, but everything was fragmented, shards of glass scattered across cedar plank floors.

And then I was inside the factory and there were cracked linoleum floors smeared with dirt and blood; rotted wooden crates piled halfway up the wall; twisted catwalks, conveyer belts, and rusted pipes; and bars on the windows creating shadows, terrible shadows.

Factory Town

I walked slowly and my feet echoed on the linoleum. And now more sounds: distant laughter, distant screaming. I looked down and saw an oversized rat scurry across the floor, and then another and another.

It was clear that the factory had been derelict for ages, nothing produced in generations. But still the workers showed up, didn't they, wearing hard hats, carrying lunch buckets and thermoses, singing *heigh-ho, heigh-ho.*

I told you you'd be disappointed, said Charlie. I told you there was nothing to see.

Why do they come here? What's the point?

No point, Russell. Tradition for tradition sake.

The Cowboy, I said. Is he here? Is this where he lives?

Certainly. Just another hundred yards or so...

And so I walked and everywhere there was death and decay and abandonment and it was all so sad, so profoundly sad.

I went through a corridor and into another section of the factory where shafts of light shone from a series of square windows. The walls all crumbling brick, and on one of the walls, in red flashpaint, the words Alive and Well. Hanging from the ceiling, from a long metal chain, a single hook, metallic and rusty. And on the hook, an old transistor radio. A preacher shouting: and it is true that the sin of this land will remain! There ain't no flood can wash it clean!

I kept walking, and on the far side of the room I came to a concrete staircase, the handrail twisted metal, and something inside of me knew it led to the Cowboy. I took the stairs two at a time, kept going

Jon Bassoff

up and up. The air was filled with dust and filth and I couldn't stop coughing. And after a long time—my legs aching, my lungs burning, my head throbbing—I reached a landing, the top story of this terrible factory. It was dark and it took several moments for my eyes to adjust, but eventually they did, and I saw what seemed to be miles and miles of rusted power equipment and empty furnaces and metal rollers and casting machines.

And then the whore was there and she grabbed a hold of my arm and said, I've been having such a good time, Russell, and you've never suspected a thing! All I do is fuck and suck, fuck and suck! So what are you going to do now? Hit me? Is that what you're going to do? Turn into your father? Make his prophecy come true?

I didn't want to argue; I didn't have the time. So I continued walking, alone, past all of the abandoned factory equipment, and then I heard a commotion coming from around the bend, some sort of a mournful chant echoing through the great rooms and corridors. I quickened my pace and saw what appeared to be a hospital bed, or at least the frame of the bed, surrounded by dozens of men, the same men with their black suits and gas masks and shovels that had attacked me earlier. Some of the men were rocking back and forth like Jews at the Wailing Wall, while others lay prostrate on the ground, praying fanatically, begging for forgiveness. Nobody seemed to hear me as I approached or, if they did, nobody paid me any attention.

The Cowboy himself lay in the bed.

He wore a cowboy hat, but the skin was gone

Factory Town

from his face, his eyes nothing but black sockets. His flesh had long since rotted and was inseparable from his flannel shirt and blue jeans. But stranger still, he was hooked up to some sort of a primitive life support system: plastic tubes splaying from his skull and neck connected to a metal box with various wires and knobs and gauge needles. On his bedside, numerous flowers and piles and piles of letters from his followers...

I pushed my way through the crowd until I was at the Cowboy's bedside. I came face to face with him, he with that fleshless grin, and still, I recognized him. One of the men in suits grabbed my hand and pleaded with me to pray, and I didn't know what to do, I had never prayed for anything in my life, and so I mouthed some words, nonsense all, and that seemed to satisfy him. Inspired by my own religiosity, the man released my hand, spread his arms into a crucifix pose, gazed up to the ceiling, and began speaking in a language that I didn't recognize. This went on for a long time, his voice getting louder and louder, the language getting stranger and stranger, and soon I realized that he was speaking in tongues, a Pentecostal believer. Well, he must have had some sort of a revelation because he started twitching and convulsing, spinning round and round in circles. Eventually he fell to the ground, and his body jerked every which way, foam rising from his mouth, but nobody stepped in to help him, a pattern in this town. Time passed and the seizure ceased, and then he popped up to his feet as if nothing had happened, continued praying, ranting.

Meanwhile, the anger was building, bile rising

in my throat. The men weren't just worshipping an idol, they were worshipping a corpse. And so I spoke because nobody else would. I spoke because I was on the precipice of sanity. He's dead! I shouted. Just leave him be! Leave me be!

I wasn't thinking; I was filled with rage. I lunged toward the corpse, started pounding on him with my fists. A lifetime of frustrations. I pounded and pounded. I pounded so hard and so long that my hands became bloody, maybe broken.

And for a long time, nobody stopped me. They were stunned, mouths ajar and eyes glazed. Then the synapses connected and the men, the Cowboy's soldiers, responded in force, locking arms and charging toward me. There was nowhere for me to go. Before I could react I was once again restrained by several of the men who then took turns striking me with fists and batons and wrenches. I collapsed into the fetal position, covering my face with my hands.

* * *

When I awakened, the men in gas masks were gone. So was the rotting corpse of the Cowboy. Head and soul splintered, I pulled myself up and sat there wobbling back and forth like a children's punching bag. I could hear the sound of water dripping on the cement, could smell the stench of burning flesh.

Disgusted, I covered my face with my hands. I touched my temple, felt the burning of the wound. As I sat there, unsure of what to do next, I heard the sound of footsteps echoing against the factory's walls, heard the faint voice of a man, the sobbing of

Factory Town

a child. I looked up. I saw a man that I recognized, Timothy Kaladi. He was still dressed in camouflage and was walking quickly across the floor. In his arms he held a child, her body covered in blankets. At first I couldn't see who she was—it was dark and her face was hidden in the shadows—but then she straightened her back, and for just a moment her eyes met mine.

Alana.

CHAPTER 21

Once again, my body failed me at the worst possible time. I tried rising to my feet, but my spine stiffened, leaving me virtually paralyzed. I attempted to call out to her, but my voice left me, a carnival mute. Alana saw me, she saw me, and she reached her arms toward me: an empty embrace. Never before had I felt so helpless. I couldn't move. I couldn't speak.

For his part, Kaladi didn't see me, his head fixed forward, and he rushed through the factory, dodging through the dilapidated machinery and equipment, leaping over scrap metal and iron ore and limestone. Alana was beautiful, so beautiful, but I could tell she was terrified. She called out to me in such a little voice: Mr. Carver…Mr. Carver…Won't you help me, sir? Won't you help me?

And then she was gone, gone into the depths of the factory, and I felt an all-consuming sorrow, a sorrow I hadn't felt in decades, not since I was a child, those terrible, terrible days...

Time passed and I heard strange violin music, long desolate notes interrupted by angry plucking. The feeling returned in my legs, and so I stumbled to my feet in search of my hope, my heart, my Alana.

I barreled through the factory, haunted by the specter of my own failures, of my own sins. And so it was that I came to an olden freight elevator, the caged metallic door badly rusted. Fingers trembling, I pressed the button and listened to the ancient parts groaning and screeching as the elevator slowly plunged through the shaft. The elevator eventually jerked to a stop, and I reached out and yanked open the caged door. Inside, a man with wild gray hair and darting eyes sat on a stool. He nodded at me. Going down? he asked in a voice harsh with disuse.

Yes, I said. I'm looking for a girl. He grunted and rose from the chair. With great exertion, he walked across the elevator and closed the door manually. Then he pressed the bottom button and we lurched to a start, falling down, down, down.

The elevator operator nodded at me. You saw the Cowboy then? he said.

Yes. But he was dead. An idol only.

No. Not dead, not dead. He lives on in you. He will never die.

The elevator continued down, and there were nightmarish echoes in the shaft, and faces, not real, pressing against the bars begging for me to let them in. There are truths, people, too terrible to reckon. Finally, the elevator slammed to a stop. The air was cold; my hands were frigid and I could see the breath from my mouth. I stood there for some time, assuming the operator would open the door, but when I glanced down I noticed that he was dead, his chin buried against his chest, blood leaking from his nose and mouth, not real, not real.

I pulled open the metal door and stepped outside. I was now in the bowels of the factory, dull light streaming in through cracks in the wall. I was surrounded by more broken-down equipment: vacuum pumps and steam engines and evaporator units. The floors were nothing but rubble. I walked slowly, my left cheek twitching uncontrollably. I didn't know where I was going, not exactly, but I knew it would be horrific, that was a certainty. All was quiet but the sounds of my shoes echoing against the tired walls.

It felt like days travelling and I had just about given up hope when I heard sounds, vague and blurry. I quickened my pace. I could now make out the echoes of children's laughter and the sound of a television show from long ago.

I couldn't figure out where the noise was coming from. Every time I moved toward where I believed the source was, it seemed to shift. I became increasingly frustrated, wandering back and forth against the wall like an asylum patient. And then I noticed a group of loose rocks at the bottom of the wall. I kicked at them with my boot, and they quickly crumbled away. I got down on my hands and knees and started pulling more rocks away frantically, my heart pounding heavy against my rib cage.

I worked feverishly, the dust and dirt causing my lungs and eyes to burn. And when the rocks were finally cleared, I dropped to my knees and peered

Factory Town

through the opening and saw some sort of a wooden hatch door, padlocked shut. I glanced around the room, searching for some type of a sharp object with which to break it open. I located a jagged piece of concrete. My fist closed over the concrete, my eyes rolled back in my head, and my body stiffened. With great emotion, I raised the concrete high in the air and slammed it down on the padlock, but the steel was too strong. Over and over I did this and then, by the will of God or the Devil, the padlock smashed open and fell harmlessly to the ground. Hands shaking, lungs wheezing, I reached down and heaved up the door, thick and heavy.

Beneath the hatch there was a wooden ladder and it seemed to extend forever. I was so lonely, so scared. Step by step I went down, and it got colder and colder, and my hands became numb making it difficult to hold on. The ladder itself was old and beginning to rot, and with every step I feared it would collapse and I would fall forever into the darkened abyss.

At some point my foot hit something solid. I glanced below and was surprised to see green grass. I had once again descended completely clear of the factory, had once again descended clear of Factory Town. I wiped myself off, rubbed my eyes with my hands. Glancing around, I could see that I was in some sort of a valley, surrounded by towering oaks and junipers. The sun was beginning to rise — how long it had been since I had seen light! — and the sky was a child's painting, all smeared yellows and oranges and reds.

For the first time in ages, the anxiety and dread that had smothered my senses began to dissipate. A hopeful smile spread across my face, and I walked down the path, a gentle breeze causing the branches to sway dreamily. I could hear the sounds of birds, living not dead. I saw a rabbit dart behind one of the trees and wait, nose twitching, and I laughed.

I breathed in the morning air, and there was no soot, no grime, no misery; I was surrounded by only peace and tranquility. And then something amazing: I touched my temple and found that my wound had healed completely. In an instant, my soul, my world, had transformed, and I continued along the path.

I walked for some time, and I came to a house, the loveliest I had ever seen. Surrounded by a white-picket fence, it was painted pale blue and was ornamented with towers and turrets and steep cross gables. The windows sloped into pointed arches and were covered by swaying white curtains. Pink star lilies lined a brick path. It was a house from fairytales. It was a house that had never existed.

Once again I heard the sound of children's laughter, now clearly emanating from the inside of the house. My heart began to race. I walked down the path to the porch. Out of the corner of my eye I saw a well-loved doll, cloth torn, eye missing, pressed against the wall. I bent down and picked it up, gripped it tightly in my hands. Then I rang the doorbell.

Voices echoed from inside of the house, and then I heard footsteps on the floor. The door opened wide and Timothy Kaladi stood there dressed in his camouflage. It took him a long moment before he recognized me, but when he did he stuck out his hand gregariously, and I shook it. Well, well, Mr. Carver, it

Factory Town

appears as if you have discovered our little hideout.

Yes, I saw you and I followed you. You were with Alana.

And she is safe. Scared but safe. I'm sure you have many questions, and there will be time for those. But for now, please, come on in. Make yourself at home. And do hurry. Before anybody sees you...

I followed Kaladi inside. The interior of the house was as majestic as the exterior. Oak pocket doors and beveled windows. Wide oak-planked floors and oriental rugs. A mahogany table with claw feet. Antique mirrors and a grand piano. A staircase with a dark wood column and ornate spindles all the way up the banister. A longcase clock, hands stopped three minutes before twelve. But the most wonderful things of all were the children. Dozens of them playing on the floor or reading on a couch or singing in the corner. And laughter. The therapeutic sound of children's laughter.

I was overcome with emotion. I could feel the tears welling up in my eyes. Kaladi glanced down and noticed the doll that I had picked up on the porch. He said: I see that you've found Charlene's little baby. She'll be ecstatic. She's been searching for that mangled doll for days.

Kaladi led me across the living room. Many of the children looked up and smiled, and a few giggled in embarrassment. I only smiled and waved politely. We walked down a narrow hallway lined with religious paintings and stained glass hangings, passing several rooms filled with more children. Finally, at the end of the hallway, Kaladi rapped a few times on a door and then slowly pushed it open.

Jon Bassoff

The room was decorated with posters of angels and unicorns, and filled with stuffed animals and dolls and figurines. Inside, three girls, who looked to range in ages from five to ten, were huddled around a board game. When we entered, they all looked up, faces glowing. Hello, Papa, the oldest one said. Who is this man you have brought?

Hello, Danielle, dear. This is Russell Carver. He's new to Factory Town. Only just arrived.

The youngest one, she with a heart-shaped face, bright red cheeks, and tight blonde curls, cowered up to the other girls. Is he the bad one? she said. Is he the Cowboy?

Kaladi smiled. No, no, of course not. He's a friend. Look, he even brought your doll. You must have left it on the porch. And you should know better than to go outside without supervision.

Charlene regarded me with suspicion. I took a few steps forward, extending the doll as a token of good will. Quickly, she leaned forward and snatched it out of my hands then sat there rocking back and forth, squeezing the doll to her chest.

How do we know? she said. How do we know he's not the Cowboy?

Charlene, don't be ridiculous. He's a friend...

He looks like a cowboy. Look at the boots he wears. He looks like a cowboy.

I shook my head and smiled. I can assure you, I said. I'm not the Cowboy. The Cowboy is dead. I saw so with my own eyes. He's only given life by his followers.

But the little girl wasn't convinced, and she sat there pouting. Maybe there's more than one cowboy,

Factory Town

she mumbled. Have you ever thought of that?

We left the room and continued walking through the house, Kaladi peeking into various rooms to check on more children. Don't worry about Charlene, he said. She's been through a lot. She tends to be suspicious of all strangers.

Alana, I said. Is she here?

Yes.

Can...can I see her?

He stopped walking and turned to face me. Are you sure you *want* to see her, Russell? Are you sure this is a good idea?

Please, I said. Where is she?

Upstairs, he said. Recovering. She too has been through so much...

Pushing Kaladi aside, I strode purposefully toward the staircase. I took three stairs at a time until I was on the second floor. I walked down the hallway, calling out Alana's name, pushing open doors, finding many children but not her.

And then, in the corner of the hallway, a small door, no more than five feet tall. I tried the handle, but it was locked. I pounded on the door. Alana? Are you in there? Open the door.

Long moments passed, and then the handle twisted and the door creaked open.

Alana stood in the doorway wearing Cinderella pajamas, head bowed, hair covering her face.

Alana...

She looked up slowly, wiping the mess of hair from her face. Then a mischievous smile spread across her angelic face.

Jon Bassoff

Hello there, Mr. Carver, she said. Hello there, Daddy.

CHAPTER 22

For a long time I couldn't move, couldn't speak. I just stared at her, and she was so beautiful, an unspoken prayer. She took a couple of steps forward, and I reached out and pulled her to me. I held her and said I love you, I love you, and I never wanted to let her go, and the tears were rolling down my cheeks.

You're safe now, I said. Nobody's going to hurt you. You hear me? Nobody's going to hurt you.

Daddy...Daddy...

Look at you! I said. You've gotten so big!

Oh, Daddy...

It's been so long, so many years, I said. I want to hear all about it. Everything. Oh, sweetheart. Everything's going to be fine now, just fine. You and me and Mommy, we're going to make a go of it. There's some joy still to be had. But not here. Not in Factory Town. Back in our old house. On Winding Brook Circle.

Jon Bassoff

We went inside the little room and sat down on her canopy bed. The walls were covered with paintings of sea animals: dolphins and octopuses and fish and turtles.

Alana laid her head on my lap, and I stroked her long blonde hair. Tell me about it, I said. Tell me all about it.

She sighed dreamily and started talking, her voice that of an angel, and she talked without pause for an hour at least, and the story was a fairy tale with plenty of witches and demons (not to mention cowboys!), but enough courageous people to keep her protected. And throughout the entire adventure what kept her spirits up, what kept the malaise at bay, was the thought of home, was the thought of her mother and me.

I asked her what she wanted to do when we got home, and she said that the only thing she wanted was to eat a big bowl of ice cream and then just sit with Mom and me. And promise you'll never let anything like this happen again! she said, looking me straight in the eyes. I couldn't bare to be away from you and Mom again.

Of course not! We'll be together from now on, and I'll never let you go, never ever never.

But happiness is fleeting at best, promises empty.

I heard a noise, very faint, from outside. Boots on the ground, marching, marching.

Sensing that I had tensed up, Alana said, Daddy? What's wrong, Daddy?

Nothing, I said. Nothing is wrong. But, still, I rose to my feet and stared out the window.

There were a hundred of them at least. The Cow-

Factory Town

boy's men. Wearing those terrible black suits and gas masks. Carrying daggers and hammers and shovels.

Daddy?

I looked at Alana and saw the fear in her eyes.

Daddy? What is it?

They're here.

Who? Who's here?

The Cowboy's men. I need you to hide. Do you hear me? I need you to hide.

But where?

The men were getting closer and closer. The window? No, too risky. Certainly they would see her.

Daddy! she said and pointed at the ceiling toward the attic door. Up there!

I didn't pause. With Alana still on it, I got behind the bed and shoved it across the floor until it was directly beneath the hatch. I leapt onto the bed and tried reaching toward the ceiling, but I couldn't quite reach it. I looked at Alana. I'm going to lift you up, I said. Alana nodded.

With one motion, I grabbed Alana by the waist and lifted her to the ceiling. After fumbling for a few moments, she managed to tug down the hatch, grab a hold of the edge, and pull herself up.

Is there enough room up there? I asked.

She nodded her head.

Okay then. Stay where you are. Don't move.

She peered down with those soft blue eyes. Daddy?

What is it?

Don't leave me here. Please.

I'll be back for you. I promise.

Slowly I closed the door, and she began to sob.

Jon Bassoff

* * *

Back in the hallway, and doors were opening and children were peeking out with worried expressions on their faces. One little redheaded boy looked up at me with pleading eyes and said, Are the bad guys here? I didn't answer him, just continued on toward the grand staircase, the muffled sounds of chaos becoming more recognizable: crying and screaming and moaning.

Slowly, I edged down the staircase, and the first thing that I saw was Kaladi lying on the base of the stairs, his body soaked in blood, his head barely hanging on to his neck. Somehow he was still blinking, gurgling up blood, and then he wasn't.

I had a hard time making sense of what I saw next. The Cowboy's men marching through the house, using hammers and daggers, slicing through throats, bashing in heads, crushing bones. And on the floor, children bloody and maimed, most of them dead, but a few of them still alive and pulling themselves across the floor, leaving smears of blood on the hardwood. But as soon as the Cowboy's men noticed any movement, one of them would march across the room, bend over the child, raise an oversized claw hammer and come down hard, crushing face and skull into an unrecognizable mess.

I watched from the edge of the living room, and none of the men paid me any mind, instead continuing on with their rampage, coldly and methodically. *There are no children in this town... The town must die with us.*

Factory Town

Outside the house, eight or ten of the masked men stood on the perimeter of the property, claw hammers in their hands, standing guard for any escapees, a narrow possibility. Meanwhile, another group of the men were using shovels to dig up the front lawn. They moved quickly and relentlessly, and within minutes had dug out a trench nearly extending across the length of the property.

Downstairs all the children were dead. I wanted to stop the men, but I couldn't. I didn't have the means. I didn't have the will. They had killed everybody. And now they were going upstairs. Where Alana was hidden.

They marched up the stairs two by two, dozens of them, their black suits bespeckled with blood, only a few remaining downstairs to continue searching through the rooms and hallways for any castaways. I could barely stand, so filled with terror. And yet I willed myself to follow them. And as I began the ascent up the staircase, I felt somebody grab my leg. I stopped and looked down. A little girl, her face bashed in, almost beyond recognition, was pulling on my leg, trying to rise to her feet. I recognized her. Charlene, the girl with the doll...

Please, she whispered, blood trickling from her mouth. Please.

And I was about to take her hand, about to hold her in my arms, when one of the men appeared. Without saying a word, he bent down, yanked the little girl away from my leg, and held her under his arm, football style. I knew what would happen next, but I didn't close my eyes in time. The hammer smashed against her head again and again and again, and then he dropped her to the floor, kicked her into a growing pile of corpses by the fireplace. And when he was finished, he nodded at me as if we were partners, as if I were an accomplice. I felt sick to my stomach. I fell to my knees and vomited. Nothing but blood. And so I was nearing the end. The wound on my temple had reappeared, the pain worse than ever, and I staggered up the stairs knowing we can't change the past, though we try for some reason.

They marched on while I followed behind. And then they came to the final room, Alana's room, and it was locked, but they used their hammers to crush through the oak door. They marched inside. I watched from the hallway, helpless as always. I wished Jesus would intervene, but he was dead; I'd seen his corpse in the factory.

There were four of them and they worked in silence, tearing apart Alana's room, piece by piece, looking for any signs of her. I had stopped breathing, and I thought my chest would explode. I had come so far, had lived through so much turmoil and torment, and now I feared that she would be taken away from me, and forever is a long time.

They finished combing the room. One of the men shook his head and walked toward the door. Another one followed after him. But the third and fourth executioners stayed behind. One of them pointed to the ceiling and I felt my heart sink.

Just as I had done earlier, they shoved the bed into the middle of the room, and both of them got on it. Seeing that they could not reach the hatch, one of the men got down onto all fours while the other one stood on top of him and pulled himself into the attic.

Factory Town

Long moments passed. I wanted to scream. There was nowhere for Alana to go. Any moment and I would see her lifeless and mutilated body topple from the hatch door.

I waited. Then I saw the soldier reappear, dropping back down to the bed below. He looked at the other soldier and shook his head. The two of them left the room. I felt I would collapse. Somehow she'd escaped. It was a miracle; there was simply no other word for it.

I was about to re-enter the room, about to call out her name when I heard a familiar voice, booming, from downstairs: Work, men, work! Get these goddamn corpses in the ground! Let his will be fulfilled!

In a trance, I walked back down the hallway and stood at the top of the stairs. Then I saw him. Michael Fennnington. We made eye contact and he grinned. Russell Carver, he said. How the hell are you? How'd you get in the middle of this massacre? Brutal, ain't it?

I didn't speak, couldn't speak.

Fennington made his way up the staircase, slowly. His white suit had been recently cleaned, but faint bloodstains remained. When he reached the top, he placed out his hand for me to shake, but I didn't move.

What you must understand, he said, is that this is for the good of us all. It gives me no great pleasure.

Dead, I said. They're all dead.

Indeed. And their bodies freed from this rancid piece of shit we call Factory Town. Their souls saved from endless torment. We're doing the right thing, Russell. Sometimes it's just hard to see.

Jon Bassoff

It's a holocaust. A goddamn holocaust.

Nonsense. We are merely following the law of the land, merely following the edicts laid out by...

The Cowboy is dead. I saw his rotting corpse with my own eyes.

Avoid blasphemy, my good sir.

Blasphemy? Fuck you. Fuck you.

But there still is the matter of Alana...

I clenched my teeth until they nearly shattered. I could feel my face redden, my body stiffen. What about her?

It seems she is still missing. Unless you have any information...

What does it matter? What does one child matter? You slaughtered the rest. Let her be.

I'm sorry. We have to finish the job. You know that as well as I.

As he spoke, I glanced over his shoulder toward the window, where outside the masked men were tossing the miniature corpses, dozens of them, into the trench in the front lawn.

I sighed and closed my eyes. I know where she is, I said.

Then you must tell me. Of course you must.

I nodded my head, took a couple of steps forward. With no hesitation, I reached back my fist and slammed into his jaw with all the force I could muster. I watched as he tumbled down the stairs, head bloodied on the wooden edges.

CHAPTER 23

I barreled down the hallway, and this was the death house, and outside all the children were buried, gone forever. My head was on a swivel, thoughts spiraling out of control, wondering what might have been.

And now when I entered Alana's room, the room itself had changed, changed completely. There was broken furniture covered with music boxes and terrifying antique dolls. The hardwood floor was all covered with clutter. It took me a few moments, but I soon realized that I was back in the bedroom of Nicole and Cory Packer. My mother. My father.

I walked slowly, the wooden planks creaking beneath my feet, until I stood in the middle of the room. The windows were open and the curtains were whipping in the breeze. I stood there for a long time and I realized that the past I remembered differed greatly from the past that I had lived...

Jon Bassoff

And then I noticed the stench, the unmistakable reek of decay. I covered my mouth and nose with my arm. My gaze shifted to the corner of the room, to the bed. At first I thought it was just a heap of blankets thrown haphazardly over the mattress, but as I walked closer, I saw that there was a figure beneath the covers. And at the top of the bed, peeking through the blankets, an arm, a woman's arm, handcuffed to the bedpost.

I walked slowly toward the bed and the blood was roaring in my skull. I reached the side of the mattress and stood there motionless, not sure if I wanted to see. But curiosity is a powerful thing, so I touched the blankets, began peeling them back.

And then I felt a hand on my shoulder.

I jumped, screamed out in terror. My father stood next to me and he was holding the *Book of Edicts*. Now, now, Russell, nothing to be afraid of. It's just me, God's humble servant.

What...what did you do?

I didn't do a thing, boy. She was the one. She was a devilish woman. Possessed by the devil himself. You'd think those vows woulda meant something, don't you think? When she promised to be true? But her promises weren't shit.

Tell me what you did!

She had her chances, son! I gave her plenty. Gave her time to repent, time to renew. But she was a whore, nothing else, and in the end she got what she wanted.

Now my voice was resigned. What'd you do, Dad? Did you kill her?

No, no. Nothing like that, son. I brought her food,

Factory Town

but she refused. I brought her water, but that was no good either. She done it to herself, you see? She starved her own self to death. And now I don't know what to do, Russell. I'm broken up by this. I'm hurting real bad.

I placed my head in my hands and tried crying but nothing came out. Nothing...

Cory Packer squeezed my shoulder tightly with his meaty fingers. Now you listen to me, boy, and you listen good. You remember the things I told you? You ain't no different than me. And there ain't no escape for you. You can run, you can fight, but there ain't no way to change who you are. You was born bad, just like your mom, just like your dad, and there ain't a thing you can do about it.

The world was dying. Right before my very eyes, the world was dying. I walked across the room, gazed out the window. An orderly was walking arm in arm with an older woman, her head shaved, her expression dreamy.

I rapped on the window, but the old woman didn't look up. She couldn't see me. Cory Packer, my father, removed a sheet from the bed. Then he dragged an old wooden chair into the middle of the room. He stepped onto the chair and, without a word, began tying one end of the sheet to the light fixture. First this world, then the next, he said.

Screams were echoing through the hallways. Screams of madness. Footsteps were banging against the linoleum. Cory Packer was working on the loose end, tying it into a Hangman's noose.

Once he was finished, he beckoned me. Suddenly, I had no control of my body. I walked slowly, in a trance, to where he stood on the chair. Then he helped me up. I faced my father, looked into my own eyes. We embraced and he kissed me on the lips. Out in the corridor I could hear the footsteps becoming louder and louder, and then I could see a shadow beneath the door. I closed my eyes and held my breath. A minute or more passed. Then I could hear the footsteps again, this time getting softer and softer until they faded away completely. I opened my eyes and Cory Packer smiled. Maybe there's a heaven for people like us, he said. But I reckon not.

He tightened the noose around his neck. He nodded at me and winked. Then, without warning, he kicked away the chair, sending me crashing to the floor. A strange sight it was, my father swinging back and forth, his hands tugging feebly at the noose, his eyes bulging wildly. I rose to my feet and stood there unsteadily, watching him swing, watching him die. I could have stopped it. I could have saved his life.

I turned around and walked out the door.

* * *

My soul had disintegrated into powder. Like in a trance, I returned to the hallway, pausing to glance at my reflection in the mirror, unrecognizable. And now I was back inside Piper Carver's house, the suburban house where I had once lived, all clean and orderly and sterile. The walls were lined with Crate and Barrel artwork, and on the far end of the hallway a photograph of Piper and me, she wearing a wedding dress, me a second-hand tuxedo. I stared at that photograph for a long time. We were both smiling

Factory Town

because we didn't know what the future held. But then, none of us know, do we?

Slowly, I walked down the hallway until I reached our bedroom. Terrible thoughts, terrible thoughts! I pushed open the French doors and stood in the doorframe, my shadow stretching across the room. The floors were all white carpet and the walls were painted pink. In the middle of the room was a crib with a butterfly mobile dangling over it. In the corner of the room was a rocking chair, and lying on the chair a dog-eared copy of a book: *What to Expect When You're Expecting*. On the dresser was an unopened package of diapers, a brand new pacifier, and a pink onesie, never worn.

My wound had reopened, and as I walked across the room, the blood dripped on the white carpet, stained forever. I was tired, so tired, so I sat down on the rocking chair and stared straight ahead, thinking about some things. I didn't know what to do, didn't know where to go, so I closed my eyes, the exhaustion paralyzing my body.

I slept deeply. I slept for days and weeks, through the changing of seasons, back through time. And then, with a sudden jolt, my eyes fluttered open, consciousness returning. I stared down at my hands and, with great apprehension, saw that I was gripping a hammer. The same hammer that the Cowboy's men had used. I lifted my head and stared, once again, at the pink wall. No longer was it blank. Now there was a name, written in big yellow letters: Alana.

Not yet born.

And now Piper was sitting at a vanity mirror combing her long blonde hair. Music was playing, a terrifying symphony, and I was suddenly good and scared. I'd been here before and knew how the scene would be played out...

Alana, my wife said. Alana...Alana...Alana. It's a beautiful name, don't you think?

Yes. It's my grandmother's name.

We'll be such a happy family, don't you think, Russell? Just you and me and Alana.

I nodded my head but didn't say anything.

And she'll become a lovely girl, full of hope and dreams, and she'll wear a cornflower blue dress.

It would be nice to think so, I said. Then I rose to my feet. The symphony was blaring louder and louder, making it hard to think. Piper turned around slowly in her chair, only it wasn't Piper anymore, it was the whore, and she was smiling mockingly, teeth sharp and yellow inside a lipstick-smeared mouth. And those eyes. Devilish. Her belly was distended, and she rubbed it grotesquely with long mannish hands. Alana, she said disdainfully.

Outside the wind started blowing hard and mean. The windows were open, and the curtains whipped around spastically. And the music...that damn music. It was pounding, pounding, causing a fissure in my brain.

I wonder, she said, whose child she is. There are so many possibilities...

The whore's eyes were bloodshot and cruel. One thing you should know. I'd never raised a hand in anger. Not once. Not once.

But now it was too late. My body wasn't mine. I was bad, just like my old man. I'd always been bad. A murderer, I walked slowly until I stood directly in front of her. I was breathing heavily, my shoulders heaving up and down. Without thinking much, I grabbed her by the wrist, yanked her to her feet. She just laughed and laughed.

Watcha gonna do, Russell? she said. You gonna hurt me? You gonna do me like your daddy said you would?

I nodded my head. Yeah, I said. Then I pulled back the hammer and swung hard, connected with the side of her head. The flesh gave, and the skull shattered.

She fell to the ground, and there was blood everywhere. The whore lay on her back gurgling blood, trying to speak, and the baby kicked inside her stomach.

I raised the hammer again, and this time I came down hard against her stomach. The whore was still alive, but just barely. *The town must die with us.* The Cowboy, my father, owned my body, owned my mind, just like he always had. I couldn't stop. I pounded her stomach with the hammer again and again and again and again. The whore moaned and cried, almost dead, and then she started pushing...

It was up to God to deliver the baby, and that he did, only she wasn't nothing but a bloody mess, and I held her in my arms, rocking back and forth, Alana, Alana, Alana, and I couldn't stop crying and thinking how there was a real sickness inside of me, and how Factory Town was where I belonged, where we all belonged.

CHAPTER 24

Outside, and it was a new day, but the sky was still dark, the frozen moon glowing beneath black clouds. I walked slowly through the empty suburban streets, and I mourned a happiness that never was. It's terrible that things had to end this way, Charlie said. Sometimes it seems like the universe has it in for us, don't you think?

I shook my head. The universe doesn't have it in for us. The universe doesn't know we exist.

Charlie smiled. Maybe you're right, Russell. It would be better that way, don't you think? Knowing that nobody is watching us? Knowing that nobody cares?

I don't know, Charlie. I don't know anything anymore.

We kept walking, and there was something calming about the desolation, the emptiness. I reached into

Factory Town

my pocket and pulled out the photograph of Alana, a computer-generated version, not real. I squeezed the photograph into a ball and tossed it onto the pavement. Charlie stopped in his tracks, bent down and picked it up.

You don't want to do that, he said. Keep the photograph.

She's dead. I killed her. A long time ago.

Keep the photograph, he repeated. The past has changed before. It might change again.

I looked at the photo and now it was clear as day. The man behind Alana, the man waiting to do her harm, was me.

After hours of walking the suburbs were all gone, and we stood in front of a lonely valley. The moon was shining, and through the trees I could see a river, shimmering. Off in the distance a lonely train whistle blew, and then I heard another sound: metal scraping against dirt.

I quickened my pace, and Charlie had a tough time keeping up with me. Take it easy there, hoss, he said. What's your hurry? You got the rest of your life to die...

Up ahead a ways, through the dark fog and mist, I could see the silhouette of a man, shovel in his hand. As I continued approaching, I saw his heavy pea coat, his red scarf. I remembered this man. He'd been digging near Charlie's house. Yes, I remembered him well...

The man stopped shoveling and looked up. A smile spread across his ashen face. There you are, he said. I was beginning to think you wouldn't show.

You talking to me?

Yes, mister. You're the only one here.

Charlie, Charlie, oh Charlie. Where have you gone, oh Charlie?

I don't understand, I said. What are you waiting on me for?

C'mon now, Russell. You've been walking an awful long time. You must be exhausted. And that wound ain't getting no better now, is it?

I touched my hand to my head, felt the wetness of blood.

What do you aim to do? I said.

When I first saw you, when you first helped me dig this here grave, I didn't know who you was. Now I know. Now you know.

I peered over the edge where he'd been digging. The hole was wide, and the hole was deep—ten feet at least. *He ain't here yet, but it's only a matter of time. Just need some mortician's wax to fill the wound.*

You got something in your pockets, he said. I suppose now would be a good time to empty 'em.

I stared at him blankly then reached into my pockets. The flowers, now crushed and putrefied.

Flowers for your grave, he said.

I nodded, tossed them on the dirt surrounding the hole.

The boy. He's already down there.

The boy?

Yes. The boy with the cape. The Annihilator. He died a long time ago. He's down there waiting for you.

I shook my head. I don't understand.

There's nothing left to understand, he said, then he raised up his arms and swung the shovel hard

Factory Town

and fast. I didn't have time to react, and the shovel slammed into my skull, sending me toppling down into the deep, dark pit.

The old man stood at the edge of the dirt, his red scarf whipping in the wind. I was beat, nearly finished. I struggled to my hands and knees and began clawing at the dirt walls, trying to pull myself up, but that only caused the walls to start collapsing.

For a long while, the man stood above the hole, watching me, not saying a word. Finally, he shook his head and said, Shot to the head. It's a fucking shame. He sighed deeply and then began shoveling dirt, tossing it into the hole.

For a while, I tried avoiding my fate, scurrying around the pit like a feral animal. The old man kept tossing in dirt, slowly, methodically. Finally, resignation. I was tired, so tired. I crawled to the corner of the hole and pulled myself into the fetal position. I squeezed my eyes shut, trying to dream. Time passed, and I could feel the dirt piling up around me. Soon I felt the dampness of the soil on my arms, on my face. I opened my eyes, and all was darkness, the nightmare of the real world.

EPILOGUE

...and then his eyes were still, too. The woman, hands trembling, chest heaving, took another step forward before her legs gave and she collapsed on the floor. And once again she became aware of the sound of the clock, the pendulum swinging back and forth, monotonously, incessantly. She pulled herself up to a sitting position and stared, once again, at the man, now only a corpse. He was flopped up against the wall, his head buried against his chest. His eyes were distended in blood-dark circles. On his temple there was a small hole, too perfect, blood smeared on the side of his face.

And then something else caught her eye. Something crumpled up in his hand. Curiosity got the better of her. Her legs still useless, she crawled across the room and pulled apart his fingers. The paper floated to the floor. With trembling hands, she picked it up.

Factory Town

It was a photograph, now splattered with the man's blood. And in the photograph, a young girl with dirty blonde hair, a pink mouth, and cornflower blue eyes. The woman studied the image for a long time. Something about the photograph wasn't right. The girl—she was too perfect. She wasn't real.

The woman flipped over the computer-generated image and saw something scrawled on the back. The writing was minute, and she had to squint to make it out:

What he did to me, I won't do to you.

The woman dropped the photo to the ground then looked up at the clock as the gears grinded and the chimes echoed.

*   *   *

In Factory Town the murderers and whores dance, feet pounding against the wooden floors, bodies thrashing against the walls and windows. Upstairs, the men sit in their plastic lawn chairs, playing cards, a game that never ends. And the Cowboy stands at the top of the factory, holding the hands of the dead, watching over the town below. Tubes and wires hang from his neck and his skull, but his eyes are open and he is smiling. He talks to whoever will listen. Even when the buildings collapse, he says. Even when the glass shatters, he says. Even when the bodies rot, he says.

Even when Factory Town dies, he says.
I'll be alive.

ABOUT THE AUTHOR

Jon Bassoff lives in Colorado with his wife and two kids. His mountain gothic novel, *Corrosion*, was called "startlingly original and unsettling" by Tom Piccirilli, a four-time winner of the Bram Stoker Award, and has been adapted for film by the screenwriter Jack Reher. His second novel, *Factory Town*, is also being adapted for the big screen.

Made in the USA
Middletown, DE
07 October 2014